HARLEQUIN
Presents

As the summer approaches we've got the reads to raise your temperature in Harlequin Presents!

Don't miss the first book in an exciting new trilogy, ROYAL BRIDES, by favorite author Lucy Monroe. *The Prince's Virgin Wife* is a tale of an irresistible alpha prince, an innocent virgin and the passion that ignites between them. In part two of Julia James's glamorous MODELS & MILLIONAIRES duet— *For Pleasure...or Marriage?*—enter a world of sophistication and celebrity, populated by beautiful women and a gorgeous Greek tycoon! *Captive in His Bed* is part two of Sandra Marton's Knight Brothers trilogy. This month we follow the passionate adventures of tough guy Matthew. And watch out, this story is in our UNCUT miniseries and that means it's *hot!*

We've got some gorgeous European men for you this month. *The Italian's Price* by Diana Hamilton sees an Italian businessman go after a woman who's stolen from his family, but what will happen when desire unexpectedly flares between them? In *The Spanish Billionaire's Mistress* by Susan Stephens, a darkly sexy Spaniard and a young Englishwoman clash. He thinks she's just out for her own gain—yet the physical attraction between them is too strong for him to stay away. In *The Wealthy Man's Waitress* by Maggie Cox, a billionaire businessman falls for a young Englishwoman and whisks her off to Paris for the weekend. He soon discovers that she is not just a woman for a weekend....

Check out www.eHarlequin.com for a list of recent Presents books! Enjoy!

Dear Reader,

Welcome to the world of the ROYAL BRIDES of USIC (United Small Independent Countries), where the members of the royal families from small countries all over the world fall in love, get married and have babies. Though perhaps not always in that order. Every story will be unique, but as the series progresses, you will see glimpses into the ongoing lives of characters from previous books.

These people populate their own world, one filled with passionate romance and the challenges of being royal in the modern world. I'm so excited about these stories and look forward to sharing with you the characters that have come to mean so much to me. I hope they find their way into your heart, as they have found their way into mine.

Blessings,

Lucy
www.lucymonroe.com

Also in the ROYAL BRIDES miniseries

Look out for
His Royal Love-Child (#2541)
June 2006
The Scorsolini Marriage Bargain (#2547)
July 2006

Lucy Monroe

THE PRINCE'S VIRGIN WIFE

Royal
Brides

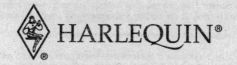

HARLEQUIN®

TORONTO • NEW YORK • LONDON
AMSTERDAM • PARIS • SYDNEY • HAMBURG
STOCKHOLM • ATHENS • TOKYO • MILAN • MADRID
PRAGUE • WARSAW • BUDAPEST • AUCKLAND

ISBN 0-373-12535-6

THE PRINCE'S VIRGIN WIFE

First North American Publication 2006.

www.eHarlequin.com

Printed in U.S.A.

All about the author...
Lucy Monroe

Award-winning and bestselling author
LUCY MONROE sold her first book in September
2002 to the Harlequin Presents line. That book
represented a dream that had been burning in her
heart for years: the dream to share her stories with
readers who love romance as much as she does.
Since then she has sold more than thirty books to
three publishers and hit national bestseller lists in
the U.S. and England. But what has touched her most
deeply since selling that first book are the reader
letters she receives. Her most important goal with
every book is to touch a reader's heart, and when
she hears she's done that it makes every night spent
writing into the wee hours of morning worth it.

She started reading Harlequin Presents books very
young and discovered a heroic type of man between
the covers of those books—an honorable man,
capable of faithfulness and sacrifice for the people
he loves. Now married to what she terms her "alpha
male at the end of a book," Lucy believes there is a
lot more reality to the fantasy stories she writes than
most people give credit for. She believes in happy
endings that are really marvelous beginnings and
that's why she writes them. She hopes her books
help readers to believe a little, too...just like
romance did for her so many years ago.

She really does love to hear from readers and
responds to every e-mail. You can reach her by
e-mailing lucymonroe@lucymonroe.com.

For Elizabeth Eakin,
otherwise known as LadyB...a fabulous reader
and one of my dear LFBJ pals.
Thanks so much for your help with naming
the country Isole dei Re for this trilogy.
Hugs,
Lucy

CHAPTER ONE

"So, were you able to hire her?"

Principe Tomasso Scorsolini paced the Hong Kong hotel suite, his cell phone pressed against his ear and waited with barely concealed impatience to discover if his prey had taken the bait.

"She came to the palace for the interview as agreed and she impressed me very much." Therese's voice rang with approval across the phone lines. "I don't know how you heard about her, but she's a sweet woman and will be good with the children. She really is ideal, but I was not certain at first that she would accept the position."

"Why?" He'd made sure Maggie Thomson had no conflicting loyalties, arranging for her current employers to dispense with her services while at the same time suggesting she consider the position in his household.

"She was concerned about the impact her leaving in a couple of years would have on Annamaria and Gianfranco, particularly in light of Liana's death."

"A couple of years? She assumes she will leave?"

"She has plans to open her own day care center after she has saved enough money. It is why she has taken positions with older children up to this point."

Ah, so she still held onto her dreams. He should not be surprised. Maggie Thomson had a stubborn streak almost as wide as his own. "What did you tell her?"

"I took your advice and introduced her to Gianni and Anna. They liked Miss Thomson immediately and she fell completely under their spell. You know how shy little Annamaria is and yet by the end of the interview, she was sitting in Miss Thomson's lap. I've never seen anything like it." Therese paused as if collecting her thoughts. "I know this is going to sound strange, Tomasso, but it was as if she was their long-lost mother…the connection between the three of them was that strong."

She didn't need to say what they both knew. The connection between the children and their real mother had never been that significant. Liana had not been a nurturer.

"That is good to hear." Very good.

"Yes, well. I told her that if she would commit to a two-year contract, we would provide her with a generous bonus at the end of it to help her with her business."

"Did that sway her?"

"Not at first. She was still concerned about the children, but I explained that when hiring domestic help, a two-year contract *was* a long-term commitment and really better than we might expect to do with someone else."

He had no plans to let Maggie Thomson go in two years, or anytime thereafter, but Therese did not need to know that. "Brilliant. And she accepted?"

"Yes."

"Good." Satisfaction filled him. "Thank you, Therese."

"It was my pleasure, Tomasso."

"Tell Claudio I will see him when I return to Isole dei Re."

"You may well see him before I do." There was something in his sister-in-law's voice that bothered him.

"Are you all right, Therese?"

"Yes, of course. Miss Thomson agreed to begin her duties immediately as you suggested."

"Very good."

"Yes, but I shall miss having the children with me."

He hadn't considered that. "I am sorry, Therese."

"Don't be silly. I enjoy their company, but it is important for them to have a more consistent caretaker in their lives. If you lived here in the palace, it would be different, but since you make your home on another island entirely, I cannot make up for their lack of a mother."

"It sounds like Maggie Thomson will do that nicely."

"For the next two years anyway."

For a lifetime if it all worked out the way he planned. "I thank you again, Therese."

She dismissed her role as unimportant and rang off.

Tomasso flipped his phone shut and smiled to the empty room. It was all coming together.

Better than even he could have anticipated, and projecting a plan's outcome was something he had perfected during his years running Mining and Jewelers.

Apparently his children and Maggie had adored one another on sight and, equally important, she was the same sweet-natured woman she had been in college. He hadn't really expected anything different since reading the report Hawk's agency had compiled on her. It also said she retained other characteristics he remembered from his college days.

According to her past employers, she was efficient, content in the domestic environment and peaceful to be around. Traits he hadn't appreciated nearly enough at the time. He'd been too interested in outward beauty to understand how much her presence meant to him…until it was gone.

He'd taken for granted how smoothly his life had run

when Maggie was his housekeeper. Four years in a volatile marriage with Liana had cured him of that complacency.

The first year after her death, Tomasso had refused to even consider taking another wife, having no desire to repeat his first foray into marital disharmony. But neither did he wish to end up like his father and for the past few months, he'd begun to crave the peaceful ease his older brother had in his marriage to the kind and even-tempered Therese.

Every time Tomasso fantasized about that kind of harmony, he could only picture it with one woman. Maggie Thomson. He could hear her gentle voice reminding him to eat breakfast before leaving the house, could remember her busy hands making sure his life ran smoothly.

He wanted that harmony again, but this time he would not make the mistake of giving her an out.

She'd walked away from him once, saying they had nothing more than a working relationship and one that had no place in her life once he was no longer her boss. He'd accepted that blatant untruth for two reasons. The first was because he knew he had hurt her and even though he'd meant to do anything but, he had felt he owed her the honor of respecting her desire to cut him from her life.

The second was that Liana had been jealous of his re-lationship with Maggie and quite vocal in her desire for him to sever ties completely with the other woman. The un-reasonable jealousy had flattered him at the time. He'd taken it as proof of Liana's passionate love for him. The idiocy of that belief still rankled.

Liana had loved only one person...herself.

He had been the means to her having the lifestyle she wanted. Nothing more. Marry a prince, become a princess. He wondered if knowledge that he was a prince would change Maggie's attitude toward him.

It did with everyone else. Which was why he had attended college under the assumed identity of Tom Prince.

He'd wanted to make relationships based on who he was, not what he was. He'd wanted to prove that he could succeed on his own, not the strength of his family name. He'd proven that, at least. He'd graduated with honors solely on his own merits, but the relationships had been another story.

Unbeknownst to him, Liana had known his royal status all along, and Maggie had walked away from the simple man Tom Prince too easily.

Would she want him as Liana had, once she knew he was of royal blood?

He conceded that it did not matter. She was exactly what *he* wanted in a wife and mother for his children. Why she chose to marry him wouldn't matter because she would still be herself, a woman eminently suitable to make his life more peaceful and to give his children the nurturing they so desperately needed.

He wasn't a fool, though.

He would not base a lifetime commitment on memories six years old. By hiring her to care for his children, he would have a chance to observe Maggie and be certain she was all that he remembered before informing her of his desire to make her his wife. He also wanted to be sure the latent passion that had existed between them had not disappeared and that it was as intense as the one scorching encounter of his memories.

He was not a man who would be comfortable with a wife who did not appeal to that side of his nature.

He refused to be like his father, finding sexual solace outside the marriage bed. He considered that behavior reprehensible and so in fact, did his father, which was why the king had never remarried after one failed attempt following the death of his first wife.

His father had called it the Scorsolini curse. According to King Vincente, Scorsolini men were fated to have one true love. Claudio and Tomasso's mother had been his. After her death, no other woman could hold his interest completely enough to ensure fidelity. He'd married Marcello's mother only months after the death of his queen because he'd got her pregnant.

He had an affair and the usually mild-mannered Flavia had gone ballistic. She had refused to be cuckolded and moved back to Italy with the young Marcello, doing the unthinkable and filing for divorce in the process. Since then, his father had had a string of mistresses.

Tomasso didn't care about his supposed fate. He *never* wanted to love like his father had and end up a widower, always searching to fill an empty void that could never be satisfied.

He knew that he was different from his father. Even a superficial passion would be enough for him to remain faithful. It had been with Liana. Though he'd believed when they married she was his one true love, he'd soon discovered differently.

Yet he had remained faithful to her despite the troubles in their marriage and his discovery that what he had thought was love was nothing more than being blitzed by her outward beauty.

How much easier would it be to maintain fidelity in marriage to a woman he respected, even if he did not love her?

"Papa will be home soon, won't he?"

Maggie smiled and tucked Annamaria into the child-size bed. "Yes, sweetie. Just two more days."

"I miss him."

"I know you do." Maggie brushed the little girl's dark curls away from her face, leaned down and kissed her forehead. "Good night, Anna."

"Good night, Maggie. I'm glad you came."

"Thank you, I am, too."

She turned off the overhead light and left the small night-light glowing before making her way to her own suite of rooms in the opulent home after checking in on Gianfranco one more time. He was asleep…finally, a small lump in the race car bed that was the same diminutive size as Anna's.

Tall for his five years, he would need a big boy bed soon. Maggie wondered if that would fall under her jurisdiction. There were so many questions she wanted to ask her absent employer, not the least of which was why it seemed the entire domestic staff looked to her for direction as if she was the housekeeper, not the nanny?

There was a housekeeper-slash-cook already, two maids and a groundskeeper besides, but they all seemed to turn to her for major decisions and she found that odd.

It was certainly different than in her last two positions, but then she was working for royalty now. They obviously had their own unique way of dealing with the domestic side of life. It felt odd, but she liked the sense of respect she got from her fellow employees and the obvious importance the prince placed on her role in caring for his children.

She closed the door to Gianfranco's room, hoping he and his little sister slept well tonight. Their father had not called as was his norm and it had been difficult settling them both into their beds. Her small charges needed her, even more than the family she had left behind.

Which was not surprising considering the fact that Gianni

and Anna's mother had died and they were both so very young, but it was shocking how much she cared already.

She loved them, truly loved them.

It should be too soon to have such deep feelings for children that she had not given birth to, but she felt an elemental connection to them and had from the moment of meeting. She'd been all set to turn down the prince's offer of employment tendered through his sister-in-law, and then she'd met the children and found she simply could not walk away from the need she sensed in them.

She'd agreed to the two-year contract, but her heart was already asking how she thought she could walk away from her small charges when her time was up. She'd been their nanny for only ten days, but in some ways it felt like a lifetime.

She'd lived in more than one foster home growing up, had had different roommates her last couple of years of college, and then been nanny to two different families, but she had never connected to anyone as quickly as she had to these two.

Except Tom Prince.

And that relationship had ended in pain for her, just as this job was going to.

From what she could tell, both Anna and her older brother spent a great deal of time missing their workaholic father. They needed her on so many levels, she was powerless to turn her back on them. Workaholic, or not, the prince couldn't be all bad, not and have such two sweet children and such a caring and obviously approving sister-in-law.

He wasn't exactly neglectful, either. He called the children daily, sometimes twice a day, and spoke to them on a level that showed he understood they were children. She didn't mean to eavesdrop, but Maggie couldn't help but overhear the children's side of the conversations.

She thought he must be a really decent father despite his preoccupation with work.

Her former employer had been much the same. It seemed to be a common enough condition among the world's truly wealthy. She'd been in her last position for two years and could count on one hand the number of major holidays her employers had spent with their children. It wasn't a lifestyle she envied, even if it meant living in luxury and extensive travel.

She'd never been interested in connecting with any of the men she'd met in the world in which she had moved since graduating from college. If she ever married, it would be to a man who knew how to be part of a family, not just provide for one.

She wanted something real, something lasting and warm…the kind of family she'd spent her childhood dreaming about.

She sighed and plopped down on the small, elegant Victorian-style sofa in her sitting room. She was twenty-six and beginning to doubt she'd ever meet a man she wanted to share her life with. That thought didn't hurt nearly as much as the prospect that because of it, she might never have children.

She grabbed the remote and flipped on the television.

She certainly wouldn't meet one in this crowd, that was for sure. She liked Princess Therese, but her husband, the Crown Prince, was every bit as focused on his work as his younger brother. Maggie doubted that would change when the couple had children and wondered if that was why they had not yet had any.

She flipped through the stations until she came across one of her all-time favorite movies—a romance made in the 1940s. She adored it and knew she'd be up until the wee hours watching it. The hero always reminded her of the one man who had made her heart rate soar into the heavens and her body feel like it was on fire.

Unfortunately, just like the man on the screen, Tom Prince had married another woman. A beautiful, sophisticated, sexy woman. The kind of woman that drew every male eye when she walked into a room. The kind of woman Maggie knew she would never be.

Tom had been her employer and housemate in college and in many ways, no matter what she'd said to the contrary when they parted, the closest friend she ever had. She'd been thinking about him a lot lately. Something about Gianni and Anna brought back memories of him and the feelings he sparked inside her.

She'd been having more of the dreams, too…the erotic ones where she relived the sensations she'd known in his arms that fateful night six years ago. She didn't understand the connection and liked it even less.

It had been hard enough losing him to Liana and learning to live without his daily presence in her life *once*. But now she felt like she was going through the withdrawal all over again and she didn't even understand why.

Determined not to think about the past and its pain, she focused on the movie, but for once, her favorite love story could not hold her attention and soon she was lost to memories she couldn't stifle no matter how hard she tried…

Maggie nervously smoothed her hands down her skirt. The letter had said casual attire for the interview, but she had wanted to make a good impression.

So, she'd pulled her long, kinky blond curls into a ponytail and pinned it into a bun, hoping she looked just a little older than her eighteen years. She was wearing a longish twill skirt, the color of wheat, and a classic white button-up blouse she'd bought at the secondhand store the year before to wear to her part-time job as a waitress.

And she'd washed all the scuff marks from her single pair of white sandals, the ones her foster mom had bought her in exchange for mowing the lawn two summers previously. Her nails were clean, but unpainted. Her lightly freckled and very ordinary features were without makeup. Which was a good thing because if she'd been wearing lipstick, she would have chewed it off her bottom lip in nervousness by now.

She needed this job. The salary listed wasn't huge, but the live-in position would make it possible for her to pursue her studies without getting another low-paying job to cover living expenses.

She rang the doorbell and took a hasty step backward when it opened almost immediately to reveal a man who was way younger than she'd expected. In fact, he wasn't much older than her. With curly black hair, a face that could have been chiseled by Michelangelo, blue eyes that would have graced an angel and a body that towered over her with finely honed muscle, he was also drop dead gorgeous.

"There must be… I think I made a mistake." She looked away from his to-die-for body and surveyed the other homes on the tree-lined street.

Had she gotten the number wrong? She pulled the paper from her purse and looked down at the highlighted address. The number was the same as the one beside the open door.

"Are you here about the housekeeping position?" Tall, Dark and Gorgeous asked in a voice that made her stomach flip.

"Um…yes."

He looked her up and down, his expression weighing. "I expected you to be older."

"Me, too."

"You thought you were older?" he asked with a gleam of amusement in his cobalt-blue eyes.

"I thought *you* would be older," she corrected, blushing.

He stepped back and indicated she should enter. "Then we were both destined for a surprise, were we not?"

"I suppose so."

"I'm Tom Prince and you must be Maggie Thomson."

"Yes. It's a pleasure to meet you, Mr. Prince."

"Tom, please."

"All right." She followed him into the living room.

"You have experience keeping house?" he asked as they took seats on opposite sides of a glass coffee table.

Remembering her years taking care of her foster siblings and ailing foster mom, she nodded with vehemence. "Lots."

Then realizing that probably wasn't as specific of an answer as he would like, she proceeded to outline her household duties for the past few years.

His expression was odd. "You took care of the house, the children and your foster mother while working a part-time job?"

"I'm good at multitasking." Hopefully that would be in her favor.

"But now that you are eighteen, you have moved out?"

"Once I turned eighteen I was no longer eligible to be part of the system. Helen couldn't get help for my living expenses, and needed me to leave so she could take another child in."

Knowing that, with all she'd given to her foster mom, Maggie still hadn't meant any more to the older woman than the money she brought in from the state had hurt. She didn't share that bit with Tom though.

His too observant and surprisingly compassionate eyes

said he'd read between the lines anyway. However all he
asked was, "The small salary is not a deterrent for you?"

"No. It would be a godsend to tell the truth. My scholarship doesn't stretch to living expenses."

"You are attending university on scholarship?"

"Yes. An academic one." As if there would be any possibility that her average build would somehow have
managed to enable her to attain an athletic scholarship. She
smiled self-deprecatingly.

"You must be very bright."

That made her shrug. Her intelligence was something
she'd always taken for granted. If she hadn't been smarter
than the average student, she would have flunked out of
high school for lack of time to study between her part-time
job and caring for her foster family. "I like school."

"What is your major?"

"Early childhood development."

He didn't laugh like a lot of people did when she told
them. For some reason, the idea of going to college to earn
a degree so she could care for children seemed amusing to
most people.

"What do you want to do?"

"One day, I want to have my own day care center."

"You should take some business courses as well then,"
he said rather bossily.

But she didn't mind. "I plan to."

He nodded his approval at this and the interview went
on from there. Surprisingly they had a lot in common.
Neither liked to watch television very much, they both
liked the same authors and they shared a similar sense of
humor. It was nice.

She would have thought she would be tongue-tied
around him, but she wasn't because although he was the

most beautiful man she'd ever met, he didn't act at all conceited or cocky about his looks.

She was getting ready to go when he said, "I have one last thing I need to discuss with you before I can make my decision."

"Yes?"

For the first time in forty-five minutes he looked less than totally self-composed. "I think we could be friends."

She nodded eagerly.

"I like you, Maggie."

"I like you, too," she said breathlessly.

He got very serious. "The position is a live-in one."

"Yes, I know. That's perfect for me."

He nodded. "If I hire you, you have to promise you'll never attempt to take our friendship beyond that. From your letter of application, I thought you would be older... I didn't think this would be an issue I would have to bring up, but I see that I must and there is no benefit in putting it off. I don't date people who work for me. Ever."

She stared at him and didn't know what to say. He seemed awfully young to have such a policy, but she certainly didn't expect him to break it with her.

When she said nothing, his expression turned even grimmer. "If I wake up to find you naked in my bed, I will fire you on the spot."

She couldn't help it, she burst out laughing. The very thought of her doing something so bold...so absurd...was more than she could take. She laughed so hard, she fell against the wall, her head shaking in negation to his comment.

Realizing that he was frowning, she forced herself to stop chortling. "I'm sorry. I shouldn't have laughed."

"I am quite serious."

That was weird, the way his speech patterns got so

formal sometimes, like the informal speak of a college student wasn't natural for him.

"You've had that happen before?" she asked with disbelief.

"Yes," he said shortly.

Wow. Bummer.

"I promise on both of my parents' graves that I will never climb into your bed, naked or otherwise."

"Both of your parents are dead?"

"Yes."

"I am sorry."

"Me, too, but thank you."

"You'll never try to seduce me?" he asked, as if there was still some doubt in his mind.

It took every bit of her self-control not to laugh again, but she managed it. "When you know me better, you'll realize what a ridiculous thought that is, but please believe me when I say that you don't ever have to worry about that kind of thing from me."

"Why, are you gay?"

She gasped and then closed her eyes, trying hard to stay collected. She opened them again. "No. I'm not gay. I'm not the type to try to seduce *anybody,* male or female," she said for good measure.

He still looked worried and she sighed.

"Look, you said you thought I must be pretty intelligent. Well, I am. Definitely smart enough to realize you are way out of my league. I don't know where you come from that you have women falling all over themselves to have sex with you, but I was raised to keep out of men's beds until I got married and that's exactly what I intend to do. Even if you were a reincarnation of John Wayne, I would not climb into your bed and beg you to have sex with me. Okay?"

"John Wayne? You lust after the Duke?"

She rolled her eyes. "Never mind who I fantasize about…just don't worry about it being you."

Suddenly a smile lit his face and she just about fell against the wall again, this time from the sheer animal impact, but managed to stay upright. Barely.

"You're hired."

CHAPTER TWO

SHE moved in a week later.

The job was an easy one. Tom was not a slob and although he was clearly used to money, he didn't require Cordon Bleu meals. She had plenty of time to pursue her studies and take care of his domestic needs. On top of that, he made her feel like his house was her home.

All she had to do was perform her job to his satisfaction and she had the run of the place. He was adamant she didn't limit her time at home to cleaning and then staying in her room. It was very similar to living in the foster care system, where she'd figured out early that if she performed well and made herself indispensable, she'd always have a home.

Mostly it had worked for her.

The only drawback to the perfection of her arrangement with Tom was the fact that she fell totally, hopelessly, forever-after in love with him. And he'd made it clear he wanted nothing more than friendship with her…ever.

His girlfriends were beautiful, sophisticated women that made Maggie feel worse than ordinary. Every single one of them underscored a truth she could not deny: even if she didn't work for him, Tom Prince would *never* look at her as anything but a friend.

Then halfway through his last year of graduate school and her sophomore year at the university, he broke up with his latest girlfriend. Instead of starting to date another drop-dead beauty, he took Maggie with him when he wanted companionship…out to dinner, to a movie, to a sports event, or even to a party.

The feelings she'd had during that month were still vivid after six long years of trying to forget.

It had been a cross between Heaven and Hell. She loved the extra time they spent together and her susceptible heart reveled in having his attention all to herself. But she never forgot his warning that he'd fire her on the spot if she tried to pursue anything more than friendship with him. Not that she would. She wasn't such a fool as to think that the change in his dating pattern meant anything special for her.

One night all of that changed, though.

She was curled up on the plush leather sofa in the living room, studying for her midterms, when he came home.

Looking totally yummy in a pair of dark jeans and Ralph Lauren sweater over a navy-blue T-shirt, he made her feel things that turned her virginal ideals on their head.

She just hoped the sensual hunger did not show on her face. "Hi. You eating in tonight?"

He dropped his books on the table by the doorway. "I thought we could both eat out."

"I wish I could," she said sincerely. "I have to study." She indicated her books and notes surrounding her on the sofa. "Midterms."

"You work too hard. You need a break."

"No, I don't." Life was easier for her now than it had been in a very long time. "You're just spoiled."

"And you are the one who spoils me." He moved closer to her, his rich, masculine scent tantalizing senses always on edge when he was near. "Let me spoil *you* and take you to dinner."

"I can't. Really, Tom. I have three tests tomorrow."

He shook his head, his expression disapproving. "You would not have so many tests if you did not take extra classes."

"I take the maximum the scholarship allows for. I want to be done early. It's better for me that way. I can start working sooner."

"If you would let me pay for your living expenses until graduation, you would not have this worry."

"No can do. What you do for me now is enough. Too much sometimes."

"You are too stubborn, you mean. And I do nothing for you that you have not earned."

"Well, since you won't be living here next year, you can't say I would be earning my keep if you provided it, could you?"

"Can you not consider it another scholarship?"

She wasn't the only stubborn one. "No."

"What are you going to do next year?"

"Get a job, or two, and find an apartment. I think one of the girls in my economics class wants to be my roommate." She hated talking about the next year, when Tom would be gone.

It hurt to know that for all intents and purposes he would be walking out of her life as easily as he had walked in. While she had a horrible suspicion she would miss him forever.

"There is no reason why you cannot stay here."

"There is every reason. It's not my house."

"It is mine and I want a caretaker."

"No, you don't. You want to give me charity and I won't accept. Please stop pushing it." She hated arguing with him as much as she hated thinking about never seeing him again.

He grinned, his expression flashing from annoyed dominant male to smiling confidence. "I am very good at getting my way."

"I noticed. I *have* lived with you for a while now."

He plucked her book out of her hand and tossed it to the end of the couch and then grabbed her wrists and tugged her up. "Then you should accept that if I want you to have dinner out with me tonight, that is the most likely scenario for our evening."

She landed with a thud against his hard male body and gasped before scrambling as far back as his hold would allow. She tried to break it, but though he wasn't hurting her in the slightest, there was no chance. "I need to study."

"You need to eat. What can that hurt?"

"We'll be gone too long. You never just go eat somewhere."

"So, maybe there is a movie playing that I want to see…you need a break. I said so."

"And because you said so it must be true?"

"Yes, this is true."

She rolled her eyes. "You're awfully arrogant for a man who isn't even twenty-five."

"I was bred to it."

"I guess." She never asked about his background because he made it clear it was not a subject he wished to discuss, but it didn't take a rocket scientist to know he came from major wealth.

"Why don't you ask one of your friends to go to the movie with you?"

"I am. I am asking you."

"I'm your housekeeper."

"You are also my friend."

Maybe…but somehow she didn't see them exchanging

phone calls and Christmas cards after he finished graduate school and moved on. And that was what decided her. She had only a finite amount of time left in Tom Prince's life. She needed to take advantage of it.

"All right. I'll study when we get home. Please tell me the movie is an early showing."

"Your wish is my command, little Maggie." He sealed his promise with a kiss.

On her lips.

He'd never done that before.

The logical part of her brain told her that kind of salute was common for him, even if she'd always been adept at avoiding any sort of touching between them.

But her body had other ideas, and lips that had kissed only one other boy before him went instantly soft against his, parting in an invitation that was as old as time and equally unmistakable. Being the natural predator that he was, he accepted the deepening of the kiss with alacrity.

His tongue slipped between her lips and slid along hers. She'd dreamed of tasting him, but no dream could compare to the rich ambrosia of his mouth. His lips and tongue explored her with such effective mastery, she moaned in pure pleasure. He made a feral sound low in his throat that sent shivers throughout her body, and pulled her forward, tugging her hands around his hips.

Her fingers convulsed in his sweater, gripping it so tightly it would have ripped if it hadn't been so well made.

His hands came around her and pressed against her tailbone, bringing her into intimate contact with his lower body. She felt his rigid length hard against her belly, but couldn't quite work out in her brain what it meant. She was too busy being devoured by an expert kisser. And loving it.

Some small part of her sanity remained and the muffled

voice of reason asked her what she thought she was doing, but she had no answer. A far more strident voice, that of unrequited love, told her she would never have such a chance again. It urged her to experience all of him that she could.

Her heart and her clamoring body demanded compliance to that voice.

Tom did something with his hand against her back and her knees buckled.

Suddenly she was tumbling backward and he was going with her. She landed with one hip on the sofa and one hip off. Her equilibrium wasn't up to keeping the balance and she and Tom tumbled to the floor. She landed on top of him, but amazingly he'd kept their lips locked together. He growled and flipped her under him, his hard thigh settled between her legs. She went utterly still, feelings rushing along her nerve endings that made her tremble and yank her head away from his.

It was too much.

She clamped her lips shut on a tiny whimper, but it escaped anyway.

He looked down at her, the angles of his face drawn with an emotion she did not recognize. "Did I hurt you?"

She shook her head, unable to speak.

"You whimpered."

She stared up at him, mute, her legs separating just a tiny bit in an involuntary gesture that she immediately tried to rectify, but could not. He had settled more firmly between her legs and pressing her own back together only had the effect of hugging his masculine thigh tighter to her.

She gasped and closed her eyes against the disgust she knew would be in his. She'd promised never to do this, but it was as if her brain had lost control of her body and it had a definite will of its own.

The fact that it was following her heart did not help her self-control.

"Open your eyes, Maggie," he demanded in a tone she doubted many people would have the strength to disobey. "Look at me."

She steeled herself to deal with his anger and opened them. "I'm sorry," she managed to whisper.

Far from being angry, his eyes were heated with a look he'd never directed her way before. "Why?"

Her gaze slid to his lips before returning to his eyes. "For kissing you."

"I kissed you."

But she had invited more. She'd been the one to open her mouth. She simply shook her head, unwilling to put her culpability into words.

"You want me." He sounded as if the thought had never once occurred to him, but she could still see no evidence of anger that she had broken their agreement. "Since when?"

She turned her head away, her pride refusing to give him an answer. The sofa was so close she could see the grain of the leather, but as a distraction from his presence it failed miserably.

He tugged her chin with implacable fingers until she was once again looking at him. "I want you, too."

"You do?" she asked in utter shock. "That's not possible."

He laughed and moved against her, making her aware of more than just the hardness of his thigh. "I'd say it's very possible."

As the implication of what she felt sank in, she blushed hot crimson.

He laughed again and then his mouth lowered over hers. This time, it was he that demanded entry to her mouth with his tongue. The kiss was incendiary, burning her sense of reality to ashes around her.

All she could do was feel. Every touch was new for her, every caress a step into an unknown but amazing world. One where passion ruled and desire was a tangible presence surrounding her.

He traced the curves of her face and neck with barely there fingertips. But when he reached her breast, his touch changed, growing more insistent and he cupped her soft curves possessively through the thin fabric of her worn flannel shirt. It was so intimate, she shuddered from the impact while he growled his approval of her braless state.

He began to knead her with a knowing finesse that made her ache in her most private place.

She needed to touch him, too, wanted to feel his skin with no barriers between them. She yanked his T-shirt out of his jeans so she could get her hands under it and his sweater. His skin was hotter than she expected, emanating warmth that made her fingertips burn deliciously.

And the hair on his chest was silky smooth. She touched everywhere she could reach, exploring his tight body with hungry innocence. When she found the nubs of his hard nipples, she stopped and circled them with her thumbs, then brushed over them, primal delight shimmering through her at his passionate response.

She was only vaguely aware of him unbuttoning the front of her shirt and peeling it back.

She noticed when his hand touched her bare skin though. Her whole awareness was consumed with the feel of his hands on her bare flesh, as her nipples hardened almost painfully and small goose bumps broke out on her flesh.

He kissed along her jaw and down her neck. "You're so soft, Maggie, so delicious."

Her only response was another soulful whimper as his mouth found her breast and then a scream as he began to suckle the nipple. Her hands fell to her sides, thudding against the carpet. She twisted her head back and forth as a mewling sound came from her throat that she could barely recognize as herself.

Then speech burst forth from her, words she did not plan on uttering tumbling from her lips in a breathless cascade. "Oh, wow! I knew it would be wonderful, but this beats anything. I feel so much, like my whole body is buzzing from a beesting."

He laughed, pulling his mouth from her nipple. "I will gladly sting your petals and drink your nectar with my tongue."

The erotic words shivered through her and she moaned.

He smiled darkly and went back to sucking her tenderized flesh. She tried to arch off the floor, but his body held her down.

"Tom…that's so good, oh, it feels so *good*…" The word drew out long and low on a moan she didn't even try to stifle.

She wasn't sure how it happened, but he lost his T-shirt and sweater and then she felt his bare skin against hers. It was amazing and things were happening inside her she'd never experienced before…a feeling of spiraling tension she didn't know how to handle. It just grew tighter and tighter and then he unzipped her jeans and slipped his hand inside.

His fingertips trespassed the top of her panties, touching her mons and then slipping between her swollen lips to caress her sweetest spot. Something happened inside her. It was like a rocket exploding and she screamed as her body bowed with unbearable pleasure.

"That's right, *bella*. Let me feel your pleasure."

She stared at him, her body convulsing as his fingers continued their ministrations. Who was Bella? Her thoughts splintered as one fingertip barely slipped inside her and he pressed the heel of his hand against her clitoris, prolonging the bliss.

He pushed further inside and she felt a stab of pain at the same time as he said, "Maggie!" his voice laced with stunned disbelief.

"You are a virgin?" he demanded as he withdrew his hand from her body, but his hand remained in possession of her most private flesh.

"Yes."

Something strange flashed in his eyes and he started whispering in a language she didn't understand and pressing kisses all over her face and throat. Overwhelmed by sensation, she didn't realize what was happening until he started pulling her jeans off.

"Tom?"

"What, *bella?*"

His use of the other woman's name again brought her back to herself with a jarring thump. Of course he was thinking she was another woman. He wouldn't want *her* otherwise, but she couldn't give him her virginity on such a pretext. *Could she?*

"What are you doing?" she asked stupidly.

He laughed, the sound husky and strained. "Making love to you."

But it wasn't love. It was sex and she didn't know if she could go through with it. "I'm a virgin."

"I know."

"I mean I'm not on the Pill, or anything."

He had her jeans down to her knees and he tugged them to her ankles. "I have condoms."

"But…" She put her hand down to shield herself even though she was still wearing panties. "Please, Tom. Wait."

He stopped and looked at her, his expression frightening in its intensity. "You do not want to go all the way?"

"You called me Bella."

Uncomfortable chagrin flashed in the depths of his cobalt blue eyes, confirming her fears she was a substitute for another woman. "Well…yes. You need me to explain?"

"No!" The very thought of hearing about some other woman he had loved while she lay practically naked below him was repugnant. "Absolutely not."

Now he looked confused. "Then what is the problem?"

Was he really that dense? "I don't want to make love with you while you're thinking of one of your girlfriends."

"I would never do such a thing," he said, his whole body going stiff with affront.

She wished with all her might she could believe him, but what had he just been doing if not that very thing?

Driven by fear of playing substitute and what making love would ultimately entail physically, she said with pure honesty, "I'm not ready."

"I think you are."

"You said you'd fire me if I ever tried to seduce you. What would happen if we had sex right now?" she asked.

His expression turned grim, disappointment flashing in his blue eyes. "It would no doubt ruin a good friendship," he said cynically.

Despite her protests, that was not what she had wanted to hear. Pain lanced through her. "I guess you're right. It would be stupid to make love, then. I can't afford to lose my job over a single night of lust."

She hated saying the words, no matter how true they were.

He jerked back from her, an impenetrable emotionless

mantle settling over him. "I will not push you into doing something you believe would be damaging to you," he said stiffly.

"I know that."

He did not reply, but moved to sit on the sofa. She could not see his expression because his head was down and his big body shuddered with several heavy breaths.

Without the passion to lose herself in, she became embarrassed and quickly redressed. She stood up, awkward and unsure what to say.

After a few seconds, even his breathing was under control. When he looked at her, there was nothing in his gaze to tell her what he might be thinking. He simply sat there in silence with his hands dangling between his jean-clad legs.

"Tom, I, uh…"

"If I found you naked in my bed, I would not fire you." That was all he said and then he got up and walked out of the room without another word.

A second later, the front door opened and shut and she was completely alone in a house that seemed to echo with all that had not been said.

Had he really wanted her?

Who was Bella?

She took his place on the couch, tears burning her eyes. Had she just avoided a monumental mistake or made the worst one of her life?

Those questions along with his words played inside Maggie's head throughout the following week.

They popped into her consciousness first thing when she woke up in the morning and bedeviled her throughout the day and then made it hard to sleep each night. When she did sleep, she dreamed of him and the pleasure he'd given her.

She would wake up aching between her legs and craving

him. Her desire for him grew to unbearable heights. Two things held her back from jumping into his bed: the memory of him calling her by another woman's name and the fact that he was rarely around. Being honest with herself, she had to admit that if the latter were not the case, the former probably wouldn't even matter.

He hadn't dated a Bella that she'd known of, but when Maggie had stayed on as caretaker of his house the past summer, he had gone home. He could have dated anyone then. Had he fallen in love with Bella and she dropped him?

It would explain why he hadn't been as focused on his relationships with women this year, why he'd only had one girlfriend and he'd broken up with her when she started getting serious. Maggie hated the thought of being a substitute for another woman. However, the temptation to try to capture his affection for herself through passion became more irresistible with every passing day. Particularly as Tom grew more distant and spent less and less time around her.

He wanted her and he'd practically invited her to his bed. Those were two facts she simply could not dismiss from her mind.

Finally the fear of losing what she did have of him decided for her. It was after eleven already and Tom wasn't home. He'd called and said not to worry about dinner, that he had a study group he was going to. On a Friday night. Like he had ever attended one of those before. He was avoiding her and she couldn't take it any longer.

She'd known it would be hard to watch him walk away at the end of spring, she hadn't known it would be impossible to live in the same house and lose what she had of him anyway. Right or wrong, she was going to sleep with him and she just hoped it would regain the closeness they'd shared before the encounter in the living room. It was worth any risk to have a future with the man she loved…even knowing that future might be extremely short-lived.

She donned her nightgown, nowhere near bold enough to actually climb naked into his bed, and turned out the house lights except one in the hall. Then she walked into his dark, empty bedroom with her heart pounding a mile a minute. She had no idea how she would have survived doing this if he'd actually been home.

The prospect of him finding her in his bed seemed much less daunting than to have to go to him and explain what she wanted. He was smart. He'd figure it out.

Even so, she got beneath the covers gingerly, feeling like a thief or something. But he had told her he would not fire her if he found her naked in his bed. She clung to that thought as she snuggled into his pillow, inhaling his scent. They would be intimate tonight and then this awful, empty void inside her chest would be gone.

As she lay there waiting for him, her week of sleepless nights caught up with her and unbelievably, her eyes grew heavy. Her last memory was looking at his digital clock to see that it was now after midnight.

She woke up to whispered voices on the other side of the bed. The mattress dipped at the same time as the small bedside lamp was clicked on and she gasped at what the light revealed.

Tom had his hand on a woman's shoulder. A gorgeous brunette with deep brown eyes, her blouse unbuttoned to reveal perfect curves encased in black lace.

"Maggie, what are you doing here?" Tom demanded, his blue eyes wide with shock, his hair obviously mussed from what they'd been doing before coming into the room.

"Sleeping," she blurted out blankly.

An explanation for her motives in being there was totally beyond her and Maggie's heart shattered while the beautiful brunette looked at her like a particularly nasty bug caught under her shoe.

The light of understanding dawned in Tom's blue gaze and along with it a wary chagrin that hurt as much as his new girlfriend's sneering regard.

"Maggie, I…" For the first time in eighteen months she saw Tom Prince at a total loss for words, but his girl-friend wasn't.

"Why is your housekeeper sleeping in your bed?" she asked Tom, her voice laced with suspicion.

"I forgot to tell her I was coming home tonight. It's wash day. Her bedding must have been unavailable." As excuses thought off the top of the head and given without the least advanced warning, it was a pretty good one.

However, the knowledge he didn't want the other woman to know Maggie might have another reason for being in his bed burned through her like acid.

The beautiful woman's lips pursed in disapproval. "I should think she'd sleep on the sofa, then."

"Yes. I should have," Maggie said with quiet dignity. She stared at Tom, her eyes accusing. "It was a big mistake to come in here."

"The timing was unfortunate," he replied, a wealth of meaning in his words.

"Most unfortunate," the brunette agreed. "However, the problem can now be rectified, can't it?"

"Of course." Maggie climbed from the bed, glad she'd worn her white cotton gown.

If she'd been naked, she wasn't sure she could have survived the humiliation. As it was, she felt angry and mortified, tears burning the back of her throat. She'd been such an idiot not to realize a man like Tom Prince wanting her could only be a temporary aberration.

Refusing to justify herself, and frankly incapable of saying another word, she spun on her heel and rushed from the room. She sprinted down the hall to her own room and rushed inside, slamming the door and locking it before collapsing on the floor and giving into the pain mushrooming inside her.

She'd been so stupid to think he really wanted her. She'd thought he was avoiding her because he couldn't handle the fact she'd said no, when in fact he'd simply found another woman and had been spending time with her. Her foolish dreams mocked her with painful indictment.

But he hadn't bothered to tell her he'd found someone else. Probably because in his mind it wasn't someone "else" but merely someone. What he'd said hadn't meant anything more to him than a reassurance about her job after the embarrassing debacle the week before. His comment hadn't been an invitation at all. It couldn't have been, not with him going out with another woman immediately after.

It had all been a product of her overactive imagination. Nothing more. But he shouldn't have said it if he didn't mean it. It wasn't fair. Maggie felt like she was going to be sick, but she swallowed down her bile. Instead, for the first time in years, she let the silent tears flow.

In that moment, she hated Tom Prince as much as she loved him.

CHAPTER THREE

THE next morning, Maggie woke feeling like she had an empty hole in her chest. Her relationship with Tom was irrevocably altered and she knew now without the shadow of a doubt that her feelings for him could never be returned. There would always be another beautiful woman waiting around the corner for men like Tom Prince.

She would have to find a roommate sooner than she had expected...and another job. It wouldn't be easy, most of the part-time jobs that worked around student hours had been filled at the beginning of the year, but she had no choice.

She walked on silent feet into the kitchen, not wanting to wake the other occupants of the house. Unfortunately, Tom was standing near the coffeepot waiting for it to finish brewing when she entered.

He eyed her warily. "Good morning."

"Is it?" she asked in a flat tone. She supposed for him, a highly sexed male whose sexual fast had ended the night before, it was.

He winced. "I am sorry about last night."

"Are you?"

"Yes. It was unfortunate."

"That's one way of putting it."

"I did not mean for you to be embarrassed that way."

Was that all he thought had happened? That she'd been embarrassed? She wished. He'd broken her heart and, like Humpty Dumpty, not all the king's horses and all the king's men could put it back together again.

"Liana doesn't know you came to my bed to make love. She believed my excuse last night."

"It was a clever story. You think fast on your feet in these situations. Are you sure you haven't had a little practice at it?" she asked with unusual cynicism.

And did he really think that it would make her feel better to know the other woman saw her as such a noncompetitor that she'd swallowed the story whole?

"Do not be sarcastic. Please. It is not like you and I have said I am sorry."

"And that is supposed to make it all better?"

"Yes," he informed her with breathtaking arrogance. "We did not have a relationship. I broke no promises. You should not be so upset."

Pain that should not be possible considering how numb she felt in her misery sliced through her. "No. We didn't...don't have a relationship, but you told me you wouldn't fire me if I came to your bed."

His face cleared as if finally he understood what was upsetting her. "And I will not," he said as if he deserved a medal or something. "It was a simple misunderstanding."

She shook her head at his misreading of the situation. "I'm going to be looking for another job today."

He frowned in irritation. "You cannot."

"I can."

"Not over this. There is no reason. It was a foolish mistake we would both be better off forgetting."

"There is every reason. *I* can't forget it. I'm sorry."

"I do not want your apology. I want you to stay on as my housekeeper."

"How can I?"

"You are being unreasonable. You have no reason to be embarrassed or want to leave. As far as I'm concerned, last night never happened."

"Does Liana know that?"

"I did not mean—"

"I know what you meant."

"It is inappropriate for you to comment on my private life in that way."

"Pardon me. I guess it's a good thing I'll be looking for other employment, then, isn't it? I'm obviously not as discreet as you need me to be."

"This morning is an aberration. One I intend to forget."

Just like she had been forgotten when a beautiful woman had come along to usurp her in his sexual desires.

"Have you considered it will not be so easy to find another job?"

"Yes."

"At least agree to stay until you find something else."

"Fine."

She'd ended up staying until the end of the semester as she'd originally planned, because finding another job to work with her tight school schedule had been impossible. But things changed between them.

She still took care of the domestic side of his life, but she spent a lot more time on campus, at the library and with the few friends she'd made. She now prepared most of his meals ahead of time and left instructions for heating. When he wanted Liana to dine with him, she made the extra portions without complaint, but never shared another meal with him herself. Not even breakfast.

Thankfully Liana was not a local college student, so she wasn't there often, but her presence could be felt in the daily constraint between Tom and Maggie.

When he asked the other woman to marry him, Maggie was not surprised, but being prepared for it did not soften the blow, and her heart bled.

He invited her to the wedding and she told him they didn't have that kind of relationship, that she didn't plan to see him again after school ended for the summer. He was her boss, not her friend and when school got out, he would no longer be even that.

For once, he had not stubbornly insisted on getting his own way, which said all she needed to know about how he really saw her.

She'd worked out a job and living arrangements by the end of the semester and moved out a week before he did. She did not bother giving him her new address and did not ask for information on where he planned to live after graduation.

She would not be able to handle seeing him married to the other woman, but she hoped he was happy. She loved him too much to ever wish otherwise.

She attended the graduation ceremony though, sitting high in the bleachers where he would not see her watching him receive his master's degree with honors. He'd worked hard to be at the top of his class.

She clapped enthusiastically when his name was called, but was gone from the stands by the time the graduates left their designated seating to join the crowd.

She'd never seen Tom Prince again, but she'd never been able to forget him, either.

Some women only fell in love once, or so she'd been told, and she figured she was one of them. He'd married a woman worthy of his incredible looks and dynamic personality, but there was a part of Maggie's heart that would always belong to him.

Maggie had only been asleep for about forty-five minutes when the feel of a small body climbing into either side of her bed woke her. She opened her eyes. "Gianni?"

"Anna got scared, Maggie. She wants to sleep with you."

The little girl snuggled up to Maggie's back, giving credence to her brother's words.

"And you do, too?"

Gianni nodded in the shadowy dark of the room. "I had a bad dream."

"I miss Papa," Anna said from behind Maggie.

Maggie was too tired herself after staying up with her memories and the movie to argue. She merely cuddled them both close and slipped back into sleep herself.

However, two hours later, after the third small and pointy elbow poked a sensitive body part, she carefully climbed out of her bed and went in search of somewhere else to sleep.

Both children were sleeping too soundly for her to willingly wake them and put them back in their own bed, but she wasn't sure what to do with herself.

Their beds were much too short for a grown person, even a woman of her no more than average height. The Victorian-style sofa in her sitting room was no longer than a love seat and no better a proposition. To her knowledge, the only other bed made up was in the master suite.

She stumbled sleepily down the hall to Anna and Gianni's father's room. He would never know she'd slept there. She'd get up in the morning and wash the sheets and replace them and when he returned the next day, he would be none the wiser.

She tossed the extra decorative pillows from the bed onto the floor and slid between the sheets. There was something vaguely familiar about the scent on the pillow where she laid her head, but she was too tired to work out what it was.

Tomasso let himself into his home quietly, forcing a brain muddled by lack of sleep and other things to remember the alarm codes to allow his entry without setting off sirens. He'd pushed himself mercilessly for the last five days so he could finish his business early and come home. He missed his children and he was impatient to see Maggie again, to find out if she was all that he remembered.

He'd gone totally without sleep for the last thirty-six hours, catching only a catnap on the plane between bouts of work. He didn't want to go into his office for a couple of days and that meant getting ahead on everything. He'd taken meds for the motion sickness he got flying when he was too tired, and then forgotten he'd taken them and had a glass of wine with his dinner and a neat Scotch whiskey an hour later.

He'd never been drunk in his entire thirty years, but he thought this graceless fumbling was as close as he had come to doing so.

Nevertheless, he scaled the stairs with a sense of anticipation and relief he had not felt in a very long time. Tomorrow Maggie would learn she was working for him. He had no idea how she would react to that news, but now that she was bonded with the children, he did not believe her first reaction would be to quit her job.

He had planned it that way of course, doing his best to stack the odds in his favor, like he did with any business deal. Unlike his first marriage, where he had allowed lust and foolish emotion to cloud his judgment, he planned to approach the situation with Maggie from the same perspective he did business. With cool, calculated reason and an intent to win.

Regardless of how she reacted to learning she was working for Tom Prince again, or that he was really Principe Tomasso Scorsolini of Isole dei Re, he had no intention of letting her walk away from him a second time.

He dropped his briefcase in the study connected to his bedroom and his carryall in the room beyond. He pressed a small button on the panel beside the door and low-level recessed lighting came on. Even so, it felt glaring to his bloodshot eyes. He was never taking that antinausea medication again.

He was loosening his tie as his gaze landed on the pile of pillows on the floor. His foggy brain could not work out why they would be there. His staff was impeccable and his children far too respectful to have had a pillow fight in his bedroom, even assuming the new nanny would let them.

Frowning over that mystery, he peeled off his jacket and hung it over the suit valet while his gaze skimmed the rest of his room. As it landed on his bed, he stopped still in his tracks.

The bed was occupied.

Who would have the temerity to invade his sanctuary? No woman he knew could make it past his security and his staff were too loyal to help any woman intent on snagging a royal lover and/or husband.

And no one, man or woman, would have been expecting him to sleep in his bed tonight. As far as anyone but his personal security team and pilot was concerned, Tomasso was still out of the country on business.

He moved closer to the bed to get a closer look. He had to brush back the mass of curling blond hair to reveal the woman's features. He did it carefully, so as not to wake her.

Disbelief warred with a feral sense of purpose as his brain identified the intruder.

Maggie.

What was she doing in his bed?

Memories of another bed, another time washed over him.

They'd shared a scorching kiss and he had come very close to making love to her. But she'd been a virgin and she'd hesitated at the last step. He'd wanted her so badly, he was shaking with it, but she had chosen her job over him.

His ego had taken a blow and he'd been both disappointed and angry, but he'd told her he wouldn't fire her if she changed her mind. Then he'd spent the next week avoiding her and trying to get his libido back under control.

He'd seen their passion as a mistake and was acutely grateful she'd refused to go all the way once he cooled down. Maggie hadn't been his type back then. She was too ordinary, too innocent and sweet. He went for gorgeous women with sophisticated tastes and a similar outlook on life. He'd thought that was what he wanted, but he'd learned that kind of woman came with a cost.

It was one he would not pay again.

He wanted the simplicity and kindness the woman in his bed had once represented in his life.

One night, six years ago, she had climbed into his bed by way of invitation, but he'd brought Liana home with him and in doing so lost any chance he'd ever had with Maggie.

She was in his bed again. A wholly unlooked-for second chance to rectify the mistakes of the past.

His brain told him there was something wrong with that scenario, that she didn't even know she was working for him, so she could not be extending any kind of invitation here. Her presence in his bed was no doubt explained by something as prosaic as the excuse he had made up to tell Liana six years ago.

But he didn't like that logical conclusion.

Okay, so his brain was a bit fuzzy, but even he could see that Maggie Thomson's presence in his bed was fate. She belonged to him. He should have seen it before. She even bore his name, or a derivative of it, but it meant she was his. Of course it did.

No. Wait. He was supposed to test her out…to see if she fit his life as well as she had before.

But how better to test her than to share her bed? That was important. It was key, even. He already knew from Therese that Maggie and his children were a good fit.

His mind worked sluggishly with arguments for and against sharing the bed with his new nanny while he finished undressing, but in the end it was physical exhaustion that decided him. He was too tired and muddled to worry about finding another place to sleep. She'd opted to use his bed. She could share it.

He slid naked between the sheets. He'd never worn pajamas. He wasn't about to start tonight. Yet as tired as he was, he did not immediately go to sleep, but turned to watch Maggie's soft features in repose. Her lips were slightly parted, perfect for kissing.

Would she mind if he kissed her good night? He was a prince. Of course she wouldn't mind. He'd never had a woman deny him a kiss, not once.

He slid toward her, his tired body reacting to her sweet feminine fragrance with surprising strength. By the time he was close enough to kiss her sleep-relaxed mouth, he was hard and aching, his body taut with need.

He pressed his lips to hers in a chaste kiss.

Her eyes opened and she looked at him as if he were an apparition. "Tom?"

"Yes, little Maggie." Tomorrow would be soon enough to explain who he was.

She relaxed again, as if his presence did not bother her at all. Her eyes slid shut. "That was nice," she whispered.

So he kissed her again, and this time she responded with drowsy generosity, parting her lips further so he could find his way inside.

He kissed her with his tongue, tasting the mouth that had haunted his dreams for far too long. She moaned softly against his lips and her small hands began exploring his body the way they had that night six years ago. He deepened the kiss with passion he hadn't felt for too damn long. She tasted perfect, she felt perfect, and he craved her like he'd never craved culmination with a woman before.

But even as confused as his brain was with exhaustion and the combined effects of the alcohol and the meds, he knew there was something not right about this.

Calling on the last vestiges of his sanity and self-control, he broke the kiss. She made a sound of protest and pressed kisses along his jaw, searching for reconnection to his mouth. His body jerked with need as her hand drifted down his stomach and brushed the hair above his sex.

"Maggie, *bella*….do you know what you are doing?"

Her eyes stayed closed, but her lips curved in a sensuous smile. "Oh, yes. I'm kissing you." And she did it again, this time right on his mouth with unerring accuracy.

He forced himself to break contact again. "Who am I, *bella?*"

"Tom." Her brows drew together in a frown. "Don't call me Bella. I don't like it."

"All right."

Her eyes opened, only a slit, but he could see the gray of her irises. "Kiss me again, Tom. I like it when you kiss me…and do other things."

The woman was a minx. Even though she talked like a wanton, she had an air of innocence that tantalized him. Her touches were not those of a woman who had pleased many men and knew how to do it. That knowledge excited him more than if she'd wrapped her fingers around him and brought him to climax.

"Is it safe?" he made himself ask, not sure if he could stop if she said *no.*

"It's always safe with you. Only you," she whispered against his lips and kissed him again, sending her tongue to mate with his in untutored enthusiasm.

Satisfaction surged through Tomasso.

Like him, she remembered how good it had been and she wanted it again too.

This time though, she was no frightened virgin. He had no regret at the thought. He wasn't sufficiently in control of himself tonight to initiate an innocent and had, in fact, never done so before. He had no desire to improvise with his brain at best in marginal control of his body.

She ran the tip of her tongue along his bottom lip and he lost it, flipping her beneath him and devouring her mouth with a need that had gone unmet for too long. Maggie went stiff as if unsure what to do, but soon she was kissing him back with a passion that undermined any desire he might have to take it slow.

He touched her everywhere, stoking her arousal and reveling in the feel of her soft feminine flesh under his fingertips. Impatient with the impediment of her pajamas, he yanked them from her body with an economy of movement.

She shuddered against him as their completely naked flesh met for the first time.

He rubbed his rigid sex against the silky curls at the apex of her thighs. "I want you so much, *tesoro mio.*"

She gasped against his lips, her body going still. "This isn't a dream."

Tomasso laughed low in his throat. "Oh, yes, it is. A dream it has taken too long to see reality."

"But…"

He kissed her again, but her body was stiff and unyielding against him. Was she going to turn him down again? Memories of his frustrated desire six years ago haunted him. No. She could not. She wanted him, her response had been too headlong and he would have her. It was meant to be.

He leaned up on one arm and cupped her breast. The nipple beaded instantly and he brushed it with the palm of his hand. She arched into his touch, while he smiled inwardly in triumph. He set about arousing her with all the skill he had at his disposal, which was considerably more than he had had at the age of twenty-four.

Liana had made love only when seduced, withholding her passion until he coaxed it from her body every single time. If there was one thing he knew about making love, it was how to tempt a woman to desire.

Maggie came to full consciousness as Tom touched her breasts with knowing caresses that drew forth the passion-

ate need she'd kept locked deep in her soul for six years.
She didn't understand what Tom was doing in her bed,
where he had come from or how he had gotten there. But
none of that mattered right then.

This was the man she loved and he was touching her in
the way she'd dreamed about for so long. It was unreal, and
yet she knew it was real. It didn't matter if it made sense, it
was happening and she was glad it was happening. Her trip
down memory lane earlier had left her vulnerable and aching
emotionally. Only this man could fill that emotional need.

And for whatever reason he seemed to want to fill it. He
wanted her. Every touch on her body told her so. Every
caress that drew forth desires she'd denied so long, proved
that he felt the same things. She didn't understand how it
could be so. He had married Liana.

He had married Liana.

Maggie tore her mouth from his, this time her entire body
writhing to be freed.

"No. We can't. You're married."

He groaned. "Yes, move like that. It's so good."

"No!" She smacked his shoulder with her fist. "You
have a wife."

He stilled and then he said in a voice she could not
doubt. "No, I do not."

Before she could ask what had happened, or anything
else, his mouth again covered hers.

Liana was gone. No one stood between her and her six-
year-old dream. The need to be loved, to belong to someone,
was so strong in Maggie in that moment, it was a screaming ache inside her. She hadn't felt this needy since her
parents' deaths. Was it the realization that she wanted a
family and might never have one, or the acceptance that she
never had…not since death had taken them away?

She didn't know what, but she wanted the hollow lone-liness to be filled. Just this once and only with this man. When his fingers slid between her legs, she didn't fight the intimacy. She remembered too well the pleasure he was capable of giving her and let her legs fall open to his touch.

He made a sound of approval against her lips as his fingers encountered the slick and swollen wetness there. Her dreams often left her like this, but tonight was not a dream. No matter how it had come to be, Tom Prince was in her bed and he was making love to her with even more effective caresses than her memories or her dreams had ever been able to conjure.

His mouth moved down to her breasts and he tortured the rigid peaks until she was shuddering with the intensity of her feelings. She didn't know what to do, so she did nothing...but he didn't seem to mind. His body was quite obviously excited and his enthusiasm made her feel beau-tiful even when she knew she wasn't.

She arched under him, needing something for which she had no name.

He lifted his head from her breasts. "Do you want me, Maggie?"

"Yes, yes, I want you so much..."

His expression glowed with victorious light and he parted her legs with a deliberate move that she could not mistake. She did not fight him. She did not want to. Soon, he would be inside her and they would be one and she would not be alone anymore.

He poised above her for a short breath and then surged inside her with one swift thrust.

Pain tore through her feminine center and she cried out, instinctively trying to buck him off.

"Yes!" he shouted as he thrust against her again, stretching tissues unused to penetration and holding her hips with hard hands.

Once again his mouth came down over hers, the quality of the kiss as out of control as his body surging over hers. Tiny zings of pleasure radiated from her core, but they could not compensate for the pain, and she felt tears sliding down her temples even as her lips returned his kiss.

That part at least was good.

He bucked and shuddered above her, a primal groan tearing from his throat and erupting against her mouth. His body went completely rigid and then relaxed, falling over her like a huge, heavy blanket.

It didn't hurt quite so much anymore, but a sense of incompletion gnawed at her. It was horrible, as if a huge crystal promise of pleasure had shattered into jagged edges that were cutting at her nerve endings. She couldn't believe she'd waited twenty-six years to experience *this*.

And she was having a hard time breathing under his weight.

She pushed against his chest. "Tom…"

He lifted his head, his expression dazed. "Are you done?"

Done? Yes, she was definitely done. "Yes," she said in a choked voice she could not hide. "I'm done. Please, *move*." She pushed against him again.

He rolled onto his back. "I am too heavy." His words were slurred, as if he'd had too much to drink.

He reached for her and she flinched, but he didn't seem to notice. He was strong and simply pulled her body into his side before his breathing pattern slid into one that indicated he'd fallen asleep. Just like that.

He'd made love to her, brought her into full womanhood and gone to sleep without so much as explaining how the heck he'd come to be in her bed.

CHAPTER FOUR

MAGGIE lay next to him for what could have been minutes or hours…she was too enervated to gauge the passage of time with any accuracy. Her entire being was in complete and utter shock.

She had just made love with Tom Prince and she could not believe it. Could not believe he was here, in her bed…or that she had allowed him to touch her and welcomed him into her body when she had never permitted another man to take such liberties.

She'd woken up fully aroused, shivering with a need she'd had no idea how to assuage. And apparently he didn't either…because it wasn't. The hollow ache she had believed would leave her when they made love was a deeper, darker pit than ever before.

How long had he touched her while she'd thought she was dreaming…thought it was just another erotic nighttime fantasy like the hundreds she'd had over the past six years? She couldn't believe she'd been so stupid.

But in her defense, although she had only one truly passionate encounter with him for her imagination to draw from, the dreams were always so real, she often woke up blood pulsing from an orgasm. The only waking one she'd had in her whole life, he'd given her.

He was also the *only* lover of her unconscious fantasies. No other man would have made it past her subconscious defenses. The touch of anyone else in her sleep would have sent her waking up and screaming in shock.

But not Tom Prince.

Only tonight had been no dream and at the last she had known it. She'd made a conscious decision to make love to him, even if it had been under the influence of pleasure so intense she'd been melting from it. The stinging ache between her thighs was proof it hadn't been pure pleasure, though.

In the end, making love to him had turned out to be as much of an untouchable chimera as her hungry desire for her own family…for a place that was uniquely hers and people she belonged to, and who belonged to her, in a way no job could ever give her. The pain between her thighs was nothing compared to the one in her chest where her heart was. She hurt so badly, she wanted to cry.

The warm wetness on her cheeks told her she already was.

Questions her pleasure drugged mind had dismissed came back full force to torment her now.

How had Tom Prince come to be in her bed? No, not her bed, but her employer's bed. Her mind could not wrap around that reality. It was too fantastic…way beyond the realm of the believable.

Were the two men friends? How had he gotten into the house? More importantly, was he still married? He'd said he wasn't and she'd believed him, but should she have? Could he be trusted? She hadn't seen him in years. Maybe he'd changed, but could a man change that much?

Tom Prince had been too honorable for that kind of behavior. Was he still?

Oh, gosh…had he even known who she was when he made love to her? Had he thought she was Liana?

No…he'd called her *little Maggie,* just like he used to. He'd told her he wasn't married, but was that the truth?

Nausea rolled in her stomach at the thought of having sex with a married man, while her body throbbed with the pain of her lost virginity.

She climbed from the bed, needing to get away from the setting of her downfall.

The prince was going to fire her for sure when he found out she'd slept with one of his friends. She would have to leave the children. More anguish tore through her. She didn't want to leave them. They needed her and she needed them. She could not believe what she had just done.

She had put her job at risk for a chance at nothing but more pain.

She stumbled into the en suite where she ran a bath and soaked until the water cooled, trying to come to terms with what had happened.

She could not believe that on the one night she'd decided to sleep in her employer's bed, he had invited a friend to come and use it. Even less comprehensible to her was that the friend would be the one man in the world she would allow to touch her in any intimate way.

She remembered him asking in her dream if she was safe and she had said always with him. Only him. Because in that moment, she'd believed he was her fantasy lover, a man who visited her only in her dreams. A man she *was* safe with.

How could Tom Prince be friends with her prince? Her employer, that was…just a second.

Cold chills raced down her spine in spite of the heat of the water surrounding her. What if Tom Prince was not a friend of Tomasso Scorsolini, but was in fact the man himself?

It all made a crazy kind of sense. Principe Tomasso…Tom

Prince. What man would dare sleep in a prince's bed but the prince himself?

Surely Tom…Prince Tomasso…had known who she was when his sister-in-law hired her. Only Therese had said nothing about the past employer-employee relationship. Or had Tomasso even cared enough to ask her last name? Yes, he had cared. She'd already decided he had to be a fairly decent dad, which meant he had to have known he'd hired her.

Or did he?

There was more than one Maggie Thomson in the world. She wasn't all that remarkable in any way.

Another thought entered her mind and shoved every other one aside. Gianni and Anna's mother had died two years ago. Relief flooded Maggie in a wave that brought tears to her eyes. *Tom* was not married. He had not lied.

But why had he made love to her?

She had been dreaming at first…or thought she was, but he had been fully awake from the beginning. Or at least she assumed he had been. What if he'd been dreaming, too?

Had he gotten into the bed, not noticing someone else was there? Had he gone to sleep and then woken to her next to him and thought she was Liana, or a girlfriend? Then he had done what men like him did with their women in the middle of the night…he'd made love to her. It was all too likely a scenario, if a painful one.

He'd called her by name, but had the times he'd called her Maggie been her dream or reality?

At some point he had to have realized she wasn't the other woman, didn't he? If so, then why had he kept going? But maybe he'd thought he was dreaming the whole time. No, that didn't make sense. Nothing made sense right now.

All she knew was that he hadn't wanted her as Tom

Prince and she knew she had no chance with a royal prince. Whatever had prompted him to make love to her, he couldn't have meant it to lead to anything important. Not with her.

She couldn't think straight. She needed to calm her racing thoughts and heart and the no longer very hot bath was definitely not doing the trick. Though the ache between her legs was a little better.

She got out of the bath and dried off and then faced the door back into the bedroom with the same feeling she would have had if it led to an arena full of hungry lions. She pulled it open slowly, hoping against hope he was still asleep as she'd left him. The room was still dark, which was a good sign, and all she could hear over the pounding of her own heart was the sound of even breathing. Good.

She tiptoed into the room, the big bath towel wrapped around her, and went in search of her pajamas. Thankfully she found them in a pile on the floor near the bed where she'd been sleeping. She would have made a mad dash back to her own room then, but remembered the security cameras in the hall and didn't want to be caught by one traipsing around in a bath sheet.

She went back to the bathroom and hurriedly dressed, then she snuck out of the room, closing the door silently behind her. She turned and had to jerk to a stop or run smack into Gianni.

He rubbed his eyes sleepily. "Why were you sleeping in Papa's bedroom?"

Her stomach dropped to her toes and wanted to stay there. "You and Anna took up all the room in my bed."

"Oh. I'll go to my own bed now. I'm not scared anymore."

"All right, sweetie. But why were you up?"

"I had to use the bathroom."

"There's one off my suite."

He rubbed his eyes again, his head drooping. "I forgot."

"I see. Come on." She walked him to his bedroom, her mind racing with ways to get out of having to face Tomasso in the morning.

If he had thought he was dreaming, maybe he'd thought she was Liana…maybe he wouldn't even realize she'd been in his bed the night before. It was a long shot, but sounded good to a sleep-deprived brain still reeling in shock after her propulsion into full womanhood.

Tomasso woke with a strange sense of well-being and anticipation.

He instinctively reached out for human warmth before reminding himself that he did not have a wife or lover who slept with him any longer. Strange that he should forget when it had been two years. Then fragments of memory began to surface from the night before and his actions began to make sense.

Maggie was in his home…in his bed. He had made love to her the night before. His eyes shot open and he looked for her, but the room was empty.

Was she being discreet for the children's sake or had she even been there? Everything that happened the night before had a dreamlike quality anyway. Even his flight home, but that had not been a dream and neither had been arriving home to find Maggie in his bed.

But what had she been doing there? And what the hell had he been thinking to kiss her and seduce her like that?

He could not believe he had made love to her the first time he'd seen her in six years…or that she had let him. The Maggie he had known would never have submitted to a man's advances that quickly. And it was only because he'd been out of his head with exhaustion combined with the effect of those damn antinausea pills mixed with alcohol that he'd made any advances at all. He had not been thinking straight.

The plan had been to test how well she fit into his life, to discover if she was the woman he remembered and then find out if the passion was still a factor between them. He had that answer at least. The chemistry between them was not a problem…she'd excited him more than any other woman he'd made love to, but he didn't feel good about that.

How could he when the evidence pointed to a promiscuity he would never have suspected of her? Damn it, could the investigative reports be wrong? What woman turned over in bed and invited a man she hadn't seen in six years into her arms? *A promiscuous one,* the logical albeit cynical side of his brain insisted. She'd climbed into his bed six years ago, too…she'd said she was a virgin then, but what if that had been a lie?

Liana had lied to him, had used her sexuality to trick him into believing her emotions were more involved than her mercenary tendencies. He couldn't afford to make the same mistake twice.

But perhaps Maggie was not promiscuous so much as opportunistic, as Liana had been. Did she now know who he was and had she decided to take advantage of her new circumstances? Unless the investigative report on her was riddled with error, that scenario was the more likely one. According to it, she rarely dated and had not had a sexual liaison in the last year or was discreet to the point of hiding it completely.

Which did not explain how she had discovered his identity before his return. He'd made sure all the portraits with his image were put away but she might have stumbled upon family photos of him with the children. Had she been waiting in his bed on purpose, hoping to take advantage?

No. That theory was illogical in the face of the fact that she had not expected him home for two more nights. No one had.

But whatever her reasons had been for sleeping in his bed, she wasn't there now. And he wanted to know why. He also wanted to know why she had let him make love to her. She had not protested once. It was completely out of character, or at least it would have been six years ago. He had changed a lot in the intervening time, perhaps she had too.

And not for the better.

His superior brain spun with the possibilities but came to a screeching halt as he pulled back the covers to climb from the bed.

There was dried blood, not his, on him and on the sheet. Not a lot, but some. Had she started her monthly? Was that why she had left?

"Papa!"

The ear-piercing squeal jolted Maggie out of a sound sleep and she sat straight up in bed, her eyes popping open to the sight of her small bedmate launching herself at the tall, gorgeous male standing beside the bed.

"Hello, *stellina,* did you miss me?"

Anna threw her thin, child's arms around his neck and hugged him tight. "Yes!"

"I missed you too, *piccola mia.*"

"He missed me too," Gianni announced importantly.

"I certainly did." Tomasso bent down and swung the little boy up in his arm so he was holding both of his children, his expression filled with a fierce kind of tenderness that made Maggie's heart squeeze in her chest.

Then his gaze met hers and went blank. Her heart started pounding wildly as memories from the night before bombarded her before she had a chance to erect her defenses. And they hurt. She still had no idea why he'd made love to her, but she knew one thing for sure…he was even further out of her league than Tom Prince had been.

He could never be hers.

"Hello, Maggie."

"Good morning…" Oh, gosh, what was she supposed to call him? He wasn't Tom Prince, not really. "Um…Your Highness."

"Tomasso is fine," he said sardonically.

"Papa isn't Maggie lovely?" Anna demanded.

"She's perfect, Papa…the best nanny ever." Gianni grinned at Maggie with adoration.

She smiled back even though she wanted nothing more than to dive back under her covers and hide. She'd made love with that man last night and she could barely breathe for the memories. "It's easy to be a good nanny when you have such wonderful children to look after."

"They are wonderful children, the best," Tomasso declared.

Both children beamed at their father's praise and Maggie felt the strangest sensation near her heart. A yearning she'd never experienced when caring for her other charges. She'd always wanted her own family, but never wished that the children she cared for belonged to her. Never before, anyway.

With Gianni and Anna, it was different. She felt possessive and protective toward them. It wasn't professional and she hated how vulnerable it made her feel, but seeing them with their father and knowing she was outside that family circle hurt in a way that it should not.

"I'm sure you want to spend lots of time with just them," she said by way of a hint to get him out of her room.

The bedroom had seemed huge the first time she'd walked into it, the queen-size canopied bed in rich mahogany almost lost in the spaciousness of the bedroom area. Even a full bedroom set to match the bed, a pair of reading chairs and a marble fireplace could not make the room feel crowded, but Tomasso seemed to fill the space entirely.

And for once, the room felt overwhelmingly small to her.

He kissed Anna's cheek. "I thought we could *all* have breakfast and then go to the beach for a couple of hours."

That plan was met with screeches of delight while Maggie's heart stuttered in her chest. He wanted to spend the day together? All of them? After last night? Wasn't he going to fire her? Was it possible he didn't remember?

He had sounded slurred there toward the end. He could have been really, really tired…but maybe he'd been a little drunk. If so, it increased the possibility that he had forgotten.

Hope blossomed in her heart. Maybe it wouldn't be so terrible after all.

"Oh, Papa, really?" Anna asked with delight.

He smiled down at her. "Yes. I have cleared my desk and will not be going to the office for a few days."

Gianni whooped with glee, not a bit like a proper prince, but very much like a small boy who was thrilled at the prospect of spending time with his father.

Maggie had suspected the children's relationship with their workaholic father was a good one, but watching the evidence filled her with bittersweet joy in the man Tom Prince had become.

Both children squirmed from their father's arms to rush from the room, Gianni saying he wanted to get his new kite and Anna proclaiming she wanted to wear her favorite shorts.

Tomasso, however, did not leave.

He stood beside the bed giving Maggie an impenetrable look.

Tomasso gritted his teeth against desire he should not feel slamming through him. It was even stronger than the regret that filled his mind to the exclusion of almost everything else. He'd come a long way from the feeling of repleteness upon waking this morning. He was ashamed now for that weakness.

He was not a stupid man. In fact, he was smart enough to successfully run a multinational company and expand it to the level of being a true world competitor, but he seemed destined to make the same mistake where women were concerned. And he hated that.

Maggie Thomson had played him just as Liana had done because no matter what his plans had been before, he had little choice but than to pursue the marriage objective now. She could very well be pregnant with his child, though the fact her menses had just started did give him a better chance at avoiding another bout of emotional blackmail with his baby as the weapon.

The knowledge did not make him feel better because even the remotest possibility that she was pregnant made him vulnerable, and that made him furious. Both with himself and with her.

"If you want my help with the children at the beach, I will have to dress," she said when the silence had stretched to uncomfortable levels.

"By all means." He put his hand out to pull her from the bed, but she scooted away from him.

"I'm in my pajamas." And in a move he considered total overkill, she drew the covers to her chin.

His brows lifted sardonically, while irritation warred with the sexual desire one bout of lovemaking had not quenched. Not after a two-year drought. "You were not so shy last night," he said with some derision, not at all impressed by her belated play at modesty.

"Last night?" she asked, striving to look confused.

His anger and derision went up another notch. She was almost as good a liar as Liana, but why she should be pretending ignorance now, he did not understand. "In my bed."

"I don't know what you're talking about. You must have been dreaming." Maggie never lied and she wasn't very good at it, she acknowledged, as the words came out sounding high and uncertain rather than convincing.

Tomasso looked totally offended and absolutely unconvinced. "I was *not* dreaming."

She winced. He sounded dangerously angry as well. "Are you sure?"

"Yes," he bit out. "We had sex last night."

She flinched at the baldness of his words, at the certainty in them. Her heart contracted at another certainty…he *had* been awake and therefore, there was no excuse for what he had done. He had seduced her from the vulnerability of sleep. She could not believe it of him, but she had no choice.

Why had he done it?

"I—"

"Do not attempt to hide your behavior by pretending it did not happen. I am not such a fool." His eyes and voice were filled with chilling contempt.

"*My* behavior?"

"Perhaps you are concerned I will fire you for the blatant promiscuity you exhibited last night, but my children are much too attached to you for me to take such a drastic measure before I assess the situation completely."

"Assess it how?" she demanded in shock at his gall, while she couldn't help the relief that surged through her that she wasn't about to be fired.

"I must determine what prompted your behavior and whether or not such behavior is likely to influence Annamaria and Gianfranco in the future. I do not wish my daughter to learn such…free and easy ways."

"Such—You think I'm *promiscuous?*"

"Please lower your voice. I do not want the children or the other servants to overhear this conversation."

Other servants? So, she was nothing to him but a servant whom he'd had sex with. How convenient. And how telling. The man saw her as totally unimportant in his life. Not only that, but she'd never been more than a servant to him. Once she'd been his housekeeper, now she was his nanny. Sex aside, she was nothing to him but another well-paid domestic.

The knowledge hurt when it shouldn't, but it also made her angry. He wasn't putting last night all on her because he was some snobby prince and she was a nobody and therefore a convenient scapegoat. "I am *not* promiscuous!"

"Perhaps you do not see your actions in that light. But you came into my arms after a six-year separation without a murmur of protest."

"If that's all you're going on, what does that make you? The promiscuous prince?"

"We are not discussing my behavior. We are discussing yours and the possible detrimental effect it could have on my children."

"There will be no detrimental effect!" He had to believe her. She couldn't leave Gianni and Anna. Hadn't she lost enough in her life?

Part of her rebelled at giving him any sort of an explanation, but her fear at having to leave the two children she'd grown to love so helplessly in such a short time overrode it. "I thought I was dreaming, or it never would have happened."

"I am disappointed in you, Maggie. You never used to lie. You were undoubtedly awake last night. I was there. I know."

"Barely. I was *barely* awake," she stressed. "I *thought* I was asleep. At first I *was* asleep and by the time I was full awake, you'd done things to me that undermined my natural defenses. You seduced me!" She glared up at him, her knuckles curling whitely around the sheet, anger heaving through her in waves that drowned her fear.

"And I wasn't the only one in that bed having sex with someone they hadn't seen in six years, but *I* didn't initiate it, did I? I wasn't the one doing the seducing," she said scathingly. "How dare you accuse me of promiscuous behavior after the way you took advantage of me last night? That is just so low I don't even have words to describe it."

His eyes flashed outrage that easily matched her own. "I did *not* take advantage."

"What would you call invading a sleeping woman's bed and seducing her before she was even awake? I call it contemptible, but perhaps you've got another word for it."

"You were awake," he ground out, his anger making the emotionless façade slip another notch.

"I was not! Not at first, anyway."

"You spoke to me when I kissed you. You knew who I was. You kissed me!"

"I thought you were Tom Prince…a man in a dream."

"I am Tom Prince."

"No, you are not. You are Principe Tomasso Scorsolini

and if I'd been aware of what I was doing, I would never have let *you* touch me intimately."

"That is a lie. You did let me touch you. You asked for it…begged for my possession."

Memories of her wanton display did not improve her temper, nor did thinking how much it had hurt when she'd gotten her wish, or how empty she'd felt afterward. "You believe what you like. *I don't care.* Do you hear me? I can't believe I let you touch me, even in my dreams." She was out of control and tears burned her eyes, but she wasn't going to let them fall. She'd cried twice for this man…once six years ago and once last night. Never again. "Only a real sexual predator would take advantage of a sleeping woman. I can't believe that's what you've become."

"I am no predator." The outrage practically vibrated off him now.

"Call it what you like. I'm not interested."

"You are being entirely irrational and perhaps that is understandable considering your condition, but I will not tolerate these insults, Maggie."

"You think I care?"

"I am your employer. It is in your best interests to care."

"What are you going to do, fire me? You can't. I quit!" She couldn't believe she'd said the words.

She sucked in air around the pain they brought, but she knew she couldn't keep working for him…even if it meant staying with Gianni and Anna.

"You tried to quit on me once before and it did not work."

"It will this time."

"Not unless you want to be taken to court for breach of contract. You signed on for two years," he said with grim implacability.

CHAPTER FIVE

THE threat sent Maggie's rage to new levels.

She hopped out of the bed and stormed over to him and poked him right in the chest. "Then sue me, or send me to jail—I don't care. I couldn't live in this house with you for another two days, much less two years!"

He stared at her in shock, like she'd grown two heads or something. "You are being extremely unreasonable. I don't remember you getting like this before."

"Before what? Before you became such a sleazebag, you mean?"

He flinched as if she'd struck him. "I realize PMS is an accepted excuse for unwarranted annoyance, but you are going too far and I warn you, my patience is not limitless. Do not call me another name."

"You think I'm angry because I'm in PMS?" she asked in disbelief.

"It is the most logical explanation."

"As opposed to the fact that I find your behavior and subsequent sanctimonious attitude abhorrent? You're like a rapist who blames his victim for enticing him." Okay, maybe *that* was going a bit too far, but she was mad enough now to spit nails. "For your information, I am not in my period and I am not in PMS. I'm not even due for two weeks."

He looked dubious. "You are not?"

"No! And I can't believe you're asking about something so personal."

"What we did last night was far more personal."

"I doubt it, not for a man like you." And knowing how impersonal it really had to have been for him to react this way was like having a razor taken to the most tender spot of her heart.

His blue gaze glittered dangerously and she watched as the patience he'd said wasn't limitless snapped.

He grabbed her shoulders and asked in a voice that made her shiver, "What is that supposed to mean?"

"What do you think it means?" she asked painfully.

"Tell me, Maggie. I am very interested in your interpretation."

Something about his quiet words made her swallow her first retort—something truly nasty—and say, "I'd say it's pretty obvious. I'm not the one with all the experience."

"If that is true, then I am glad. I am not in the habit of having unprotected sex like we did last night."

"What do you mean, *if?*" she asked, newly incensed and feeling another slashing chunk ripped from her heart. If she had imagined a thousand morning-after scenarios, not one of them would have even remotely resembled this one. "I don't make a habit of lying."

"You lied when you said you didn't remember last night."

He had her there, but she wasn't backing down. She'd lied to avoid an embarrassing confrontation he had obviously been intent on having. She hadn't lied to hurt or manipulate someone else. "I only wish I could forget."

"Do you? I wonder. You lied when you said you had not started your monthly."

"I didn't! Okay, so I lied about not knowing what you were talking about. I hoped you didn't remember. Like I said, I wanted to forget it. But it's just plain dumb to think I'm lying about having my period. Why would I?" And how could he keep accusing her of it?

Maybe they hadn't been as good friends as she'd thought six years ago, because he'd never told her he was a prince. But he had to have known her pretty well after living with her for almost two years. She'd never hidden *her* real self from *him*.

"I don't know why you would lie, but I do know you are doing so. There was blood. You *must* have started."

Blood? There had been blood? She hadn't noticed in the bath, but then she'd been too busy dealing with the shock of having sex for the first time with a man she had thought forever lost to her and had never expected to even see again. "I didn't start."

"Then what was the blood from?"

She refused to answer, staring at him in stony silence.

Something about her expression must have gotten to him because his dark complexion paled. "I did not hurt you?"

"Yes, as a matter of fact, you did," she slotted in, feeling vindicated, but not one whit less devastated by the emotional pain shredding her insides.

He went positively pasty and her soft heart refused to allow her to continue the torment, no matter how much he might deserve it.

"It wasn't your fault…at least, not in the sense that you were rough with me or something. Apparently pain and some blood is inevitable."

He wasn't looking appreciably better. "Why inevitable?"

"First times hurt, or so I've been told," she mumbled, looking away.

He made such a strange sound that her gaze flew back to him. "You were a *virgin?*" He looked well and truly horrified by that prospect.

"Yes. Not that it matters. It's not an experience I plan to repeat anytime soon."

He stared at her in total shock. "No. That is not possible. You are twenty-six."

"I don't know what my age has to do with it. Women don't have an expiration date on their virginity, you know. *I am not promiscuous,*" she repeated for good measure.

He moved over to sit on the edge of her bed, almost as if his legs were not quite supporting him. Though she dismissed that thought as fanciful. Prince Tomasso was much too strong for such infirmity.

Suddenly she remembered she was standing there in her pajamas and nothing else. They weren't racy by any stretch, but the thin cotton wasn't exactly disguising, either. Her nipples were erect…she must be cold. It could not be his presence that was doing it, but it didn't matter. She didn't want him noticing.

She walked around the bed, giving him a wide birth, and climbed back under the covers. She wanted some answers and she wanted them before the children came back.

He frowned. "If you were untouched, then why did you ask me to kiss you…and do other things?"

"I told you, I thought I was *dreaming.*"

"About Tom Prince." Some of his color returned and with it a measure of his natural arrogance.

"If you must know, yes."

"But you were awake."

She shrugged. They'd already been over this.

"You are saying I took advantage of you in the basest way."

"Well, if the shoe fits…"

His jaw set as if hewn from granite and his eyes blazed at her. "I am not a sexual predator. I believed you were awake. I would not have touched you otherwise. You must know this."

She shrugged, but deep in her heart she suspected that was the truth. As real as her dreams seemed to her, she could very well have responded to him in a way that would have deceived him about her level of awareness before she ever came awake.

"You wanted me…your body was very receptive," he said confirming her thoughts.

"Not receptive enough," she muttered however, remembering the pain of his penetration.

"I did not know of your innocence. I took you too quickly."

"You shouldn't have *taken* me at all."

He contemplated her in unnerving silence for several seconds. "For you to be so receptive you must have frequent dreams of this nature with me in them."

If only he knew. "That's none of your business."

He smiled, for a moment looking so much like the man she remembered, the man she had loved, her heart ached. "You never forgot me."

"It wouldn't say much for my brain if I had. It's only been six years, not sixty, since I saw you last."

"But I think it is more than mere clinical memory…you did not want our friendship to end."

"Then why did I end it?"

His eyes narrowed and then he smiled again, this time the expression too smug for her liking. "Because of Liana."

"I suppose it boosts your ego to think so."

He considered her in silence for several seconds, all lightness draining from his expression, and a man she did not know—the prince—took over his countenance. "Or maybe this whole 'it was a dream' story is a ruse and you exchanged your virginity for the hope of a crown? You thought to trade on the guilt you knew I would feel when you told such a story? It was a good gambit, and may yet work."

She gasped, so shocked by the level of his cynicism coupled with the implication he would allow himself to be manipulated, she forgot to be angry. "Do you really believe that?"

His gaze shuttered, he stood again as if her nearness was no longer acceptable. "It is a possibility."

"My goodness, technically, so is the end to worldwide hunger, but it's the realm of *probability* that we're discussing here."

"Women throughout history have gambled their innocence on the chance of wearing a crown."

"Not in the last century, I'm sure."

"You would be surprised."

Maybe she would. This was a rarified world she knew very little about. "Nevertheless, I assume I would have to marry you to do that."

"Yes."

"Then you have nothing to worry about, do you? I can hardly force you to the altar."

"Can you not?"

"Of course not."

"If you are pregnant with my child…" He let his voice trail off, the implication of what he was saying obvious.

Maggie choked on what she wanted to say next as the prospect of pregnancy filled her consciousness to the exclusion of all else. A baby? Tom Prince's baby? No, Prince Tomasso's, but still…a baby. A family. Her own family that no one could take away from her.

Her hand slid to her stomach and she pressed against it, her heart beating much too fast as the blood drained from her head.

She couldn't be pregnant. Not after just the one time, but even as she thought the words, her knowledge of the sexual reproductive system mocked them. One time at this particular time of the month was more likely than if they made love over and over again a few days later. She could feel the horror of fearful certainty stamping itself on her features.

"I see the idea had not yet occurred to you." But a strange look of speculation on his face made her wonder if he thought it had and she was faking her shock.

Where the thought came from, she didn't know, but she couldn't shake the impression that he thought she might have done the whole thing on purpose.

She shook her head mutely, the movement making her dizzy.

"Why look so dismayed? As bargaining chips go, it's a very strong one indeed."

"Babies are not bargaining chips," she whispered, unable to believe she was having this conversation, much less what had led up to it.

She'd had sex with a prince and he thought it had been entirely consensual…which, if she was honest with herself at least, she'd have to admit it had been. She might have thought she was dreaming at first, but even after she realized she wasn't, her desire for this man had been too strong to deny.

She should probably apologize for the predator comment.

"For some women they are."

It took her a moment to remember what they were talking about…oh, yes, babies as bargaining chips. He'd made it sound like he had personal experience in that arena.

"I'm not one of them."

Too caught up in the ramifications of the night before on her own life for her to wonder what had prompted the bitter tone in his voice, she got up from the bed.

She pulled the covers with her, not caring if he thought her modesty ridiculous after last night. "Please get out of my room. I would like to dress."

"We have more to discuss."

"You're right. I have a lot of questions for you." Like how she'd come to be working for Tom Prince again. "But not right now." She didn't have the ability.

His eyes narrowed. "Very well. Carlotta will be serving breakfast in fifteen minutes."

"Eat without me. I'm not hungry."

"If you are pregnant, skipping meals is not good for the baby."

"Please don't mention that. Not…not right this second." She needed time to cope with the possibility.

"You've got the shocked and dismayed bit down pat. I have to give you that."

She stared at him. "Are you accusing me of trying to get pregnant on purpose?" she asked baldly, refusing to banter about it.

"Not accusing you, no."

But he didn't trust her. She was sure of it. Pain splintered through her. Bad enough to know she was so far from the kind of woman he would want to marry she might as well be a nun, and an alien one at that, but to have him doubt her integrity on top of that just hurt, a lot.

Without another word, she turned away, heading toward

the sanctuary of her bathroom, the sheet trailing behind her, her heart and mind in pain-filled turmoil.

"Maggie."

"Go away, Tomasso, *please.*"

"I will have Carlotta hold breakfast until you arrive."

That made her turn. "Please don't."

But he was already headed out of the room and made no indication he had heard her.

Maggie would like to have spent the day hiding in her room, but one thing that had clearly not changed about Tomasso from six years ago was his stubbornness. The man liked to get his own way and considering the fact he had been raised a prince, she understood why he was so used to it.

To think that she'd lived two years in the same household as a prince and not even known it.

Tomasso looked up when she entered the dining room, his gaze going over her with tactile strength, and her skin heated with feelings she would rather forget. He stood politely and pulled the chair out from the table beside Anna.

He smiled at her as she took her seat, nothing in his expression giving away the fact that he'd dropped the biggest bombshell of her life on her. "You look lovely."

She barely refrained from rolling her eyes as she said, "Thank you."

She'd pulled her long, corkscrew curls away from her face with a clip at the back of her head and donned a pair of slim-fitting jeans and a yellow T-shirt with matching yellow flip-flops for the beach. She was hardly dressed like one of his normal companions, being as far from haute couture as a woman could get without wearing a burlap sack.

"But I think you will be too warm in those jeans on the beach."

"I'll be fine. I'm used to the heat on the island. My last job was in Houston, Texas." Besides, she felt protected in the jeans.

The thought of prancing around in front of him in a pair of shorts—or worse, a swimsuit—after what had happened the night before made her shudder inwardly.

"That's a long way from where we went to college. How did you end up there?"

"A job. I'm sure all of that information is in my employment file."

"But perhaps I would rather hear it from you."

"And there is quite a bit I'd like to hear from you."

His eyes said he could guess at what those things were. "Perhaps that can wait until later?" he asked with a pointed look at the children.

"Yes."

"Tell me how you ended up in Houston."

"My first job out of college was with a family in Seattle. They knew the family I went to in Texas and recommended me to them." She'd hoped the move across country would help her forget Tom Prince once and for all.

It hadn't worked. Her dreams traveled with her.

"Why did you leave the first job?"

"Their youngest started high school and they felt my position had become redundant."

"You sound like you did not agree."

"High school can be a really difficult time and both parents were too busy to spend much time with their children. I felt taking away the steadying influence of the only adult in their lives that had time to be there for them was a mistake."

"Did you tell the parents this?"

"No. I'd only been with the family two years and it wasn't my place, but it's not a decision I would have made."

"You would be the mother who made sure she was available after school for her children, no matter the ages, would you not?"

Considering their conversation earlier, that question had more than passing significance. However, he might as well know from the beginning that she had no desire to be a glorified single parent. "Yes, but I would expect my husband to be just as committed to their emotional welfare."

"That isn't always possible."

"It should be."

"A man's commitments—"

"Should begin and end with his family. Everything else is filler, not the other way around."

"That's a simplistic view of life."

"Maybe," she conceded. "But it's the way I feel."

"You have very strong opinions on family for a woman who was raised in the foster care system."

"You don't have to be raised with two loving parents to know that is what is best for a child."

"Perhaps not."

"I grew up knowing my place in the family was dependent on what I did for the family. I wasn't loved. My children, if I have any, are going to know a different kind of life. They will always know they come first, that they are loved and that I don't expect them to earn my affection through work or perfect behavior. I won't marry a man who won't give them the same sense of emotional security."

There. He could put that in his pipe and smoke it. His concept of family was vastly different from hers, from what she could tell.

"What's foster care?" Anna asked.

"It's when you live with someone besides your parents as a child."

"Like we live with you?"

Maggie laughed. "No, darling. You still live with your papa. I am your nanny. I work for him. I'm not a foster mom."

"But I want you to be my mom. You would be the best." She turned to her father. "Can Maggie be my foster mom, Papa?"

"No, silly. Maggie can't be our mom unless she married Papa, and he is a prince," Gianni said. "He can't marry a servant."

The arrogant words spilling from such young lips made Maggie wince, but Tomasso merely laughed.

"You are wrong, my son. This is the twenty-first century. A man, even a prince, can marry who he likes. Your mother was not a princess and I married her."

Gianni looked at his father with eyes that reflected the same cobalt-blue. "But she was beautiful like a princess."

Pain slammed through Maggie. Pregnant or not, she could never belong to Tomasso and he would never belong to her. Because Gianni was right. She wasn't beautiful enough to be the woman in Tomasso's life. She was too ordinary for a man of his extraordinary status and personality. She could never live up to the type of woman that he was used to being around. No way could she hold his interest for a lifetime.

She'd learned six years ago that she could not even hold it for a couple of weeks.

The thought of marriage to a man who might find a more beautiful, exciting partner around any corner filled her with dread. She hadn't been enough for him six years ago and she knew she wasn't enough for him now. She was not and never would be one of the Lianas of this world.

"So is Maggie pretty," Anna staunchly defended. "Don't you *want* Maggie for a mama?"

Gianni's expression went stoic, so like his father's that Maggie sucked in a breath as her heart constricted. "Maggie is only staying for two years. She told *Zia* Therese. I heard her. A mama has to stay your whole life unless she dies like our mama did. Besides nannies are better than mamas. We get to see Maggie every day. We don't need a mama."

Guilt flayed Maggie as she realized one of the reasons for the distance Gianni sometimes kept between them.

He was a small child who had already faced the tragic loss of his mother. He knew Maggie did not intend to stay around forever and so he was trying to protect his emotions. She should never have agreed to take the job in the first place, but looking back she did not know how she could have walked away from the children after meeting them.

She also found it terribly sad, not to mention revealing, that Gianni thought having a nanny was better than having a mother.

"I don't care what you say. I want Maggie for my mama!" Anna's voice carried the conviction of a three-year-old on the verge of major meltdown.

"Perhaps you will get your wish, *stellina*," Tomasso said soothingly and then turned and ruffled Gianni's hair. "And perhaps you will learn to like the idea of having Maggie for your mother, my proud little son."

Gianni's lip quivered. "But what if she goes away?"

"If she married me, I would not let her go away."

Both children looked at their father with the kind of hope that broke Maggie's heart and filled her with anger. Didn't he realize how hurt they were going to be when that hope was disappointed?

No matter what he had said that morning, he could not

seriously be considering marriage with her. She wasn't his type and she never could be. And that knowledge had the power to wound in a way nothing else did. Not his distrust, not even his stupid male posturing about the night before.

She didn't fit in his world. She was too ordinary and that wasn't something a fairy godmother could change with a magic wand.

They went down to the beach and helped the children fly kites and then Tomasso waded in the surf with them while Maggie arranged a blanket under the large pavilion set up for the family's use on their private beach. She lay down on her stomach and watched the three play in the surf while her mind spun with the possibility of being pregnant by Tomasso.

Even if she was, he couldn't be serious about marriage. Could he? But he was a prince…maybe the thought of his child being born out of wedlock carried more weight than it did for the average modern man. Why hadn't he used protection then? Even if he had believed she was experienced, there was no reason for him to assume she was on the Pill…or even physically safe.

Far from answering any of her questions, their discussion that morning had only added more to the morass of thoughts in her head.

But overriding it all was an insidious thought that would not leave her alone. If she married him, she would be mother to his other two children as well and she would never have to tell them goodbye. She would have the family she had always longed for.

Eventually the three got tired of playing in the water and joined Maggie in the pavilion, where they built an amazing sandcastle and Maggie got to see first hand how caring Tomasso was with his two small children. For an alpha male who could cynically accuse her of using her virginity to try to trap him into marriage, he had a surprisingly tender side.

He also flirted outrageously with her, as if he was really glad to be in her company as well. In light of his accusations, it made no sense and she was careful not to let herself fall under his spell. But it grew increasingly difficult as the day wore on and she saw more glimpses of the man she'd known and loved six years ago.

He insisted on putting the children to bed together, and she felt a treacherous sense of family growing on her. But she wasn't his wife. She was his nanny…his *servant*. But then, when had she ever been anything else?

Afterward, he stopped her in the hall before she could make good an escape to her suite. "Come for a walk with me."

There were questions she wanted to ask him and the children were nowhere around to overhear the answers. "All right."

He led her out the sliding glass doors on the south side of the house and down to the path that led to the beach.

It was a beautiful night, lit by a full moon. The island breeze lifted her hair and sent it swirling gently around her face despite the clip. "I love it out here."

"According to Therese, you have been very happy here on Diamante."

"Your home is beautiful."

"It was my parent's vacation home."

"A vacation home?" While it wasn't on the level of grandeur of the palace filled with Italian marble and artwork that rivaled that of the Vatican on Scorsolini Island, Tomasso's eight-bedroom house was hardly what she would have considered a vacation cottage.

"They escaped the pressures of state here. At least that is what my father told me."

"Your mother died many years ago, didn't she?"

"There were complications with my birth." And the knowledge of that hurt him, she could hear it in his voice.

"I'm sorry. That must have been hard to know growing up."

"No harder than knowing both your parents were gone."

"They didn't die until I was eight years old. I had enough years with them to know what I want to give to my children by way of a home."

"Yes, I suppose you did. Was there an accident?"

"Yes. I survived. They didn't."

"We have that in common." She knew he meant he had survived his birth while his mother had not.

"Yes."

He looked back over his shoulder and flashed her a smile.

Her heart contracted and she tripped, barely catching herself before pitching forward into him. Thankfully the path to the beach was well lit and lined with a curling wrought-iron railing. She grabbed it and held on as she continued walking. "The children said that there are diamond mines on this island."

"Yes. The island is named for them."

"Does that mean there are ruby and sapphires on Rubino and Zaffiro?"

"No. Those islands were named with some poetic license. However, we have discovered lithium on Zaffiro. Soon, the mining operations and jewelry stores will rival the shipping company for contribution to Isole dei Re's GNP."

"You should be very proud of yourself."

"I am not the operations."

"But you drive them."

"Therese said something?"

"Your children love to talk about their wonderful papa."

"And you feel I spend too little time with them?" he correctly guessed.

"Since you are asking…yes."

"And the fact that a whole country's GNP is impacted by what I do away from them—?"

"Means that your job is important, not that it is more important than them."

"You and the children share a strong rapport."

"Maybe it's too strong."

"Why do you say that?"

"They will be hurt when I leave. You heard Gianni this morning."

"As I told my son, perhaps I will not let you leave."

"You can't marry me just because of one lustful mistake."

They had reached the beach and he stopped and turned to face her, his determined expression all too easy to read in the light of the full moon. "If you are pregnant with my child, you will marry me."

CHAPTER SIX

"Don't be stupid, Tomasso."

He cupped her shoulders, coming so close their bodies practically touched. "I like the way you say my name… your American accent is cute."

She didn't feel cute. She felt hot and bothered and suspected he knew he had this immediate impact on her.

"Your accent only shows when you are agitated…or rather, I should say, the way you speak changes."

"How?" he asked, sounding genuinely interested while his thumbs drew lazy circles on her shoulders.

"You get more formal in your speech patterns, though you seem to speak more that way now, regardless," she mused, trying for a casual attitude she did not feel.

"Ah. I made a concentrated effort to blend in with the other college students six years ago, but Italian is the primary language of Isole dei Re. The speech patterns of my native tongue are slightly different than your American English."

"But everyone here speaks English." At least everyone had to her. Even the children.

"Our small country is close to the United States…there are many American influences."

"I didn't notice any on Scorsolini Island. The palace is incredible. The frescos in the formal rooms rival the Sistine Chapel."

"The Scorsolinis are from Sicily, not Rome."

"They're both Italian."

"A Sicilian is a Sicilian first, Italian second. It is the way they are made."

"That explains it."

"What?"

"The arrogance."

He laughed and the sound shivered through her.

"I used to love your laugh."

"I think you used to love me."

She turned her head away, looking out over the dark, dark sea. "What an ego you have."

"No. Merely a logical brain. There is only one man whom you would have allowed into your arms last night. Tom Prince. Why is that? Because you dreamed of me so frequently, an erotic encounter in the night could be dismissed by your subconscious as one more fantasy. That says much for how deeply you felt for me."

"I thought you'd convinced yourself I was lying about the dreams."

"I only considered the possibility you were lying to me; I was not convinced of it and now I am certain you were not."

"Why?"

"The way you responded to me last night…it was too much like a woman touching and allowing the touch of a longtime lover, not a woman making love for the first time to a man she had not seen in six years."

"And you would know the difference?"

"Yes," he said with all the arrogance she had accused him of having earlier.

"I see."

"I doubt it. You are much too innocent to do so."

"Not anymore."

"Very much innocent still. You did not experience completion, did you?"

"That's not something I want to discuss."

His thumbs moved to either side of her face, gently forcing her to look at him. "Next time it will be much better."

"There will not be a next time."

"Yes. Maggie, there will." His expression was incredibly possessive. "You belong to me now."

"No, I don't."

His lips cut off any further protest.

It was a claim-staking kiss pure and simple, but it didn't matter to her treacherous body. At the first touch of his lips, she melted into him and when he broke his mouth from hers, her fingers were clutched in the hair at his nape and her body was molded to his.

"You are mine."

She always had been, but she wasn't about to admit it to him. He was too darn confident as it was.

"I'm not the only one breathing heavily here," she pointed out.

"And your point is?"

"That if I belong to you, then you belong to me." Which wasn't something she was sure of at all, but he needed to know that she intended their relationship to be equal…even if inside she knew it never could be.

"Naturally."

She stared at him in shock. "You don't mean that."

"Why would I not? Marriage is no small step. It requires effort and commitment from both parties."

"We aren't talking about marriage here."

"Are we not?"

"You're so stubborn. That hasn't changed."

"I know my own mind."

"And think everyone else should share its leanings."

"That is not true."

She tugged out of his arms, surprised that he easily let her go. "Right."

"Maggie, you will discover that we want the same things."

"You want to give up your mining and jewelry operations to run a day care center?"

He laughed and started walking again, his body betraying none of the tension she felt.

"Did you know who I was when Therese hired me?" she asked. It was time to get some answers.

"Yes."

"Did she know you used to know me? She didn't say anything."

"I did not tell her."

"Why not?"

"I wanted you. I was not sure you would come if you knew."

"Why was it so important I accept the position of nanny to your children?"

"I had a plan."

"What do you mean, a plan?"

"A plan to find an acceptable mother for my children. An acceptable wife. When I met Liana, I was swept away. I married her because she was a beautiful, glamorous woman, but she was not a natural mother, nor did she take on the responsibilities of her position. I could not risk another such mistake by setting out to 'marry for love' again." There was scorn in his tone. "I require a wife who understands what duty is and who will fulfil her duty—to me, my children, my country. I remembered your dedication when you worked for me before...and I realized that, if you had not changed, you might well be the wife I needed. And I decided to bring you here in order to ascertain that."

As she listened to him, her mind numbed with shock. He wanted to marry her, but he did not want to love her and he made it clear that what he wanted her for most was her Girl Scout loyalty and willingness to serve. She could not imagine a more mundane, less romantic beginning to a relationship. A less successful one.

"You've got to be kidding."

"I do not joke about things this important."

"But you can't choose a wife based on a woman's performance as a housekeeper."

She stopped and he followed suit, turning to face her again. "I am certain I could, but in this case, I planned to watch you in action with my children. The position of nanny was eminently suited to offer me a chance to test the waters and see if you were the woman I remembered and if you would have the same harmonious effect on my children's lives that you had at one time had on mine."

"I wondered why your staff seemed to come to me for decisions I would not expect a nanny to make."

"It is true that I gave instructions to place you in this role." He sounded extremely proud of his forethought.

"So, you were testing my suitability?" she said flatly.

"Yes."

"That would make your talk of marriage now a bit premature, wouldn't it? I mean, don't you need to do more tests?"

"Things changed last night."

"Because we had sex?"

"Yes. I had planned to wait for that, to make sure everything else was as it should be before we tested the passion between us."

Passion, not love. He'd loved the beautiful Liana, now he wanted a marriage of convenience with the ordinary Maggie. "Then why didn't you?"

"I was not thinking straight."

"Why not?"

"I'd had no sleep for a day and a half. I'd taken motion sickness pills and then had a couple of drinks. They didn't mix well. My mind was clouded."

His explanation was no less unbelievable than his plan to test her out as a possible wife material.

"So, you were drunk?" She'd been right about the word-slurring thing. Only now it didn't feel like nearly such a hopeful prospect as it had that morning, because the connotations were far more detrimental to her sense of feminine value.

He'd only made love to her because he was out of his mind on meds that should not have been mixed with alcohol.

"Not exactly."

She wrapped her arms around her middle, but she did not feel comforted. She just felt alone. Again. "Close enough to it."

"*Sì.*"

"Did you know I was in the bed before you got into it?"

"*Sì.*"

"Then why did you?"

"The truth? I was too tired to go elsewhere."

"You weren't too tired to seduce me."

"I kissed you good night. You responded."

Even that didn't make any sense to her. "Why did you kiss me?"

"I cannot explain it. It made sense to me at the time," he said with a self-deprecatory gesture that was at odds with his usual arrogance. "You must accept that our coming together was meant to be."

"How can you say that?"

"It happened, did it not?"

"That's hardly proof that Providence was behind it. I'm not your type, Tomasso. I never could be." He had to see that. "I'm nothing like Liana."

"And I am glad of that. She brought more discord to my life than joy."

"What do you mean?"

"Marriage to Liana was not the equivalent of domestic bliss. She did not like the strictures of our duty to the crown or our people. Nor was she enamored with mother-hood, and spent little time with our children. She accused me of working too much but she was never here when I was home. The most domestic peace I'd ever known was when you were my housekeeper. Six years ago, Liana's beauty and charm dazzled me, but I am not so easily swayed by a pretty face now."

He might as well have said flat out that Maggie was far from beautiful. Which she'd known, but having it reiterated so baldly was shattering. "But what about passion?" she asked in a whisper.

"We share that…in abundance."

She wasn't so sure about that. They'd had sex because he had been drunk, for all intents and purposes, and she was there, convenient and in his bed. How real, or focused, was that kind of passion? It certainly wasn't enough to sustain a marriage to a man of his sexual appetites and stunning appeal to the opposite sex.

"Let me make sure I have this straight. You had me

brought here to the island so you could *try me out* as wife material?" Just saying the words offended her.

Tomasso had not believed she was worth courting through the usual channels. He'd had no plans to court her at all if she didn't pass his tests.

"Yes, but my behavior last night circumvented the time for any such assessment. It is lucky for me that you are so obviously well matched with my children."

"In other words, you really wanted a nanny who was willing to sign a longer contract than two years."

"Don't be foolish. Being my wife constitutes much more than merely caring for my children."

"Yes, I suppose it does. You'd expect me to warm your bed as well."

"A situation we will both enjoy."

"You couldn't tell that by me."

Instead of being piqued by her insult, he smiled with supreme male confidence. "The next time I will make you scream in ecstasy."

"Yes, well…that's not something *I* want to test right now."

He moved in closer, his scent and his presence causing a reaction inside of her she tried desperately to stifle. "I could make you want it."

"I would rather you didn't."

"Why?"

She stepped back. "Because while you are apparently convinced you've found your answer to domestic peace, I'm not nearly so certain. I signed on as your nanny and as far as I'm concerned that's all I am at the moment."

"That is not possible after last night."

"On the contrary, today showed how very possible it is."

"And if you are pregnant with my child?"

"I don't want to discuss that."

"I do. You told me you were not due for your monthly for two weeks. That makes conception a strong possibility."

"But it still isn't certain."

"It can be."

"How?"

"Tomorrow, I can take you to the doctor."

"Don't even think about it. I have no desire to be the center of a media frenzy."

"Then a pregnancy test. They are very accurate now."

"You know this from experience?"

"Liana tested her second pregnancy before consenting to see a doctor."

"Oh. Where did she get the test?" She couldn't see a princess going to the local grocery store and buying one.

"I do not know, but I will procure one for you."

She opened her mouth to argue that it would be little improvement over her going to the doctor for a pregnancy test.

He pressed his forefinger against her lips to silence her. "In secrecy."

She closed her mouth and he pulled his hand away, tracing her bottom lip with his fingertip in the process. "All right?"

"Yes. Thank you."

She turned to walk back to the house.

"Maggie."

She didn't stop walking, but looked back over her shoulder. "What?"

"If you are pregnant with my child, I won't let you go."

The next morning, Tomasso announced at breakfast that he wanted to take the children and Maggie snorkeling.

"Are you sure you need me along?" Maggie asked, even

as the prospect of snorkeling the crystal blue waters of the nearby lagoon tempted her.

She would have to be with Tomasso and his presence was much more detrimental to her peace of mind than it had been six years ago.

"But, Maggie, you said you'd love for Papa to take us snorkeling, don't you remember?" Gianni asked.

She had said that, when the children were talking about going with their father…before she'd known who their father was. "I didn't say I didn't want to go, sweetie. I just wanted to be sure your papa doesn't mind having an extra person along. After all, he's been away from you two for over a week. He might want to spend time with you alone."

"But it will be more fun if you are there, too," Anna said plaintively.

"I want you along," Tomasso affirmed in a voice that brooked no argument.

"Papa knows the best places to go. And there's nothing to be scared of in the water," Gianni said with an endearingly earnest expression. "Papa said so."

And since Papa said it, it must be true. Maggie smiled. "All right then, but you must promise not to abandon me to my own devices."

"I'll stay with you," Gianni promised.

"I as well," Tomasso said with a timbre to his voice that sent awareness arcing through her.

And he knew, the fiend. One thing she was beginning to realize. This man was more merciless than the one she had known six years ago. If she couldn't be swayed by logic, he wasn't averse to using seduction. Both were toward the result he wanted…a wife who would cause him no trouble and would care for his children.

Being thought of in those terms was not exactly flattering, but she got the impression that her opinion wouldn't carry much weight with him, either.

"Me, too," Anna piped in, so obviously not wanting to be left out that Maggie ruffled her hair and thanked her.

At least the children would be around to act as a buffer between her and Tomasso.

Forty-five minutes later, the protection she'd expected to feel in their presence was sadly lacking.

Tomasso had been giving her swimsuited body hot looks for the past ten minutes…ever since she'd taken off the shorts and T-shirt she'd been wearing over her modest one-piece. It didn't feel modest, with him watching her as if he could see right through the skin-hugging lime green Spandex.

Darn him anyway. None of it was real…this pseudopassion he insisted on projecting at her. It was just his way of getting what he wanted. Something he was really good at, but her body didn't know the difference. Her stupid, susceptible heart insisted on being affected. No matter how many times she told herself it was just his way of convincing her to his way of thinking, she still reacted as if all that hot passion was real.

She helped Anna get her last fin on with fumbling fingers and hot cheeks.

"Do you need a hand?" But his expression said he knew exactly why she was all thumbs.

"No, thank you. I've got it."

He nodded and then thankfully, climbed off the end of the boat and jumped into the water to wait for the rest of them to join him. Maggie helped the children into the water before sliding in herself to land against Tomasso's hard muscled body.

She gasped as his arm snaked around her waist and his lower body tangled with hers. *"Tomasso."*

"Yes?"

"The children."

He grinned. "They swim like fishes and are waiting right here."

"But…"

His hand brushed down her body, curving possessively over her rear before he pulled away. The man was a master seducer. "Are you ready?"

"Yes, of course." But really, she was breathless from his brief touching, and tingling in places she didn't want to mention.

"Okay, then."

They all pulled their masks down, the children doing so with such competence it was obvious they'd done this many times before. Tomasso made sure they all stayed together and Gianni had been right. His papa did know the best places to snorkel.

The water below them teemed with the vibrantly colored life of the ocean. It wasn't long before Maggie was totally lost to awareness of time or anything else. She was shocked into screaming when her body was suddenly flipped over by a pair of strong arms.

She sank and then bobbed back up, tearing her mask from her face as she did so and spitting out her mouthpiece. "You *fiend!*" she shrieked at Tomasso.

He widened his eyes with feigned innocence. "What? I was only trying to get your attention."

The children chortled where they trod water nearby, their laughter as obvious as the amusement lurking in his blue eyes.

"You could have tapped me."

"I did. Twice."

"Oh." She hadn't noticed.

"I even tickled your foot," Anna said.

"My feet aren't ticklish."

"Apparently," Tomasso said with a wicked gleam. "I wonder if that is true of the rest of you?"

"Don't try finding out," she warned, though not at all sure what she would do if he did try.

"We're hungry for lunch," Gianni informed her before his papa could say anything else provoking.

"But it can hardly be time."

Tomasso pointed to his diver's watch. "Thirty minutes past actually."

She stared at him in shock and then quickly examined each child's back for sunburn. Luckily, there was no evidence of redness, but she still felt terrible. "It's a good thing we used such strong sunblock, but I'm so sorry I kept you all in the water so long."

Gianni squirmed away from her in the water, giving her the look a child gives his mother when she's fussing. "We were having fun, too, but we got hungry."

"Yes, we were and are…for many things." The innuendo in Tomasso's words no doubt went right over the children's heads, but Maggie got it and had to fight hard not to blush at the implication.

"Daddy went swimming underwater without his snorkel. He pretended to be a shark. It was funny, but you didn't notice him under you, did you?" Anna asked.

"Uh…no."

Tomasso gave her a look that singed her to her tiptoes. "The view from down there was even better than from the surface."

She knew the seduction was just that, but this time she

wasn't even sort of buying it. She didn't believe for a minute that looking at her average figure had put that look in his eyes. "Shall we go back to the boat?"

"Sure."

Tomasso helped the children back into the boat before turning to help her, but she peddled backward. "I can get in fine by myself."

"But a gentleman always assists a lady. Isn't that right, Gianni and Anna?"

"Yes, Papa," they chorused.

"You wouldn't want me to set a poor example for my children, would you?"

Right now she didn't particularly care what kind of example he set. Only, the bigger a deal she made out of it, the more likely she was to spark awkward questions from the two small chaperones she'd been a fool to believe would make a significant difference in the way Tomasso treated her. The man had subtle seduction down to an art form.

She didn't answer, but swam forward and allowed him to lift her onto the wide step.

He kept his hands on her waist. "I do not want you wearing this swimsuit in front of other men."

"What?" The comment was so unexpected, shock coursed through her. "Why not?"

"Have you looked at yourself when it is wet?"

She didn't make a habit of looking at herself when she swam, no. She did now, peeking downward, unsure what could be putting that territorial tone in his voice and gasping in shock when she saw.

The suit was unlined, but dry it was perfectly opaque. Wet, the lime green Spandex looked painted on and see-through. Her nipples showed dark and hard against the clinging fabric, while the curve of her breasts was perfectly molded as well, and she could only be eternally grateful God had made the curls between her thighs even lighter than the blond hair on her head because there was just the vaguest shadow alluding to her feminine place.

She wrapped her arms around herself and glared. "You could have said something."

"Why? I enjoyed the view, but I do not want to share."

"I'm not yours to share, or otherwise," she hissed too low for the children playing in the boat to hear.

His dark brow rose in questioning mockery. "That is a matter of interpretation."

"No, it isn't."

"Would you like me to remove your fins for you?"

What could she say but yes, considering that to insist on doing so herself would mean moving her protective arms from her exposed body? She nodded.

He took his time, caressing his way down her calf, one hand gently massaging her ankle as the other removed the fin from her foot. His hand moved from her ankle to her foot, still massaging in a way that made even her bones tingle. "Feel better?"

"Y-yes…"

He smiled knowingly and tossed the fin into the boat before repeating the entire process with her other foot. It took far longer than she would have taken herself, but she couldn't make her mouth form words of complaint. By the time he was done, she was panting in little gasps that gave away her reaction to his touch.

He might be seducing her into accepting his marriage of convenience, but her body was more than willing to react and she couldn't seem to do a thing about it.

He winked as his hands fell away. "All done."

Swallowing, she nodded. He certainly was all done, but

if his primary objective had been to remove her gear, then she'd eat the fin he'd just tossed in the boat. The man was a walking—make that swimming—menace.

Using one hand, while her other arm remained across her breasts, she climbed into the boat. She could feel his gaze on her backside and she didn't even want to know what her wet suit revealed to him. With a sense of desperation she didn't attempt to hide, she literally dove for one of the brightly colored beach towels stacked on one of the empty seats.

She didn't even bother to dry off before wrapping the large terry sheet around her sarong style. She was never wearing this swimsuit again.

CHAPTER SEVEN

TOMASSO climbed into the boat with a grace she envied and then started the small outboard motor. He lifted anchor and then guided them to the shallows, cut the engine and dropped anchor again an easy paddle from the shore.

This time when he went to help her out of the boat, she gritted her teeth, determined to bear it in silence. She'd given him far too much reaction already today, but she couldn't stop her heart from racing.

Her initiation into intimacy had been painful, but her body chose to remember the pleasure before penetration as well as the mind-numbing completion he'd given her six years ago. She craved closeness with him, both physically and mentally. It was as if the last six years had never happened and her emotions were as tightly wound up in him as they'd ever been before. How could something so devastating happen overnight?

Her desire-befuddled brain had no answers, but nor could it deny that a profound change had occurred inside of her. Her heart had once again made a place for Tom Prince…or Prince Tomasso. It didn't matter what she called him, her heart knew he was the one man who would ever reside there.

It wasn't fair that he should have such an impact on her and she have no defenses against it, except to pretend indifference when she felt anything but. But life was not fair, and she'd learned that long before she'd met him the first time.

With the children's help, she spread out a blanket under the shade of the dense island foliage further up the beach and then laid out the lunch. Once they'd eaten, Anna and Gianni cajoled Tomasso and Maggie into a game of tag. Afterward, she was only too happy to lay down on the blanket in the shade with the little ones and take a lazy nap.

She woke to the feeling of something soft brushing across her stomach. Her eyes slid open and she saw that Tomasso was seated on the blanket beside her, sweeping a palm frond across her sensitive flesh. Her now dry, but still thin bathing suit was no barrier to the riotous sensations he seemed intent on evoking.

She realized the towel was no longer wrapped around her at the same time as the palm frond took a dangerous sweep upward, trespassing the valley between her breasts. "What happened—"

His fingertip pressed against her mouth. "Shh…the children are still sleeping."

And they were, looking so angelic, it made her heart ache.

The palm frond continued its tantalizing touching and she put her hand on his wrist to stop him, but part of her didn't want to.

His fingertip slid from her lips to the rapidly beating pulse in her neck. "I want you, Maggie."

"No."

"Yes. And you want me, too."

She wanted to say no again, but her mouth refused to utter the lie. Though a certain amount of fear mixed with that desire. Would it hurt again?

"No."

"I didn't ask a question," she whispered.

"Your eyes did."

"What question was that?"

"You are afraid it will hurt again, but I promise you, it will not. Had I known of your untouched state the first time we made love, I would have done all that I could to avoid giving you pain then."

She couldn't help noticing he had not said he regretted touching her, though. "It has to hurt, doesn't it…the first time?"

"Perhaps, a little. But there are ways of making the pleasure so great, any pain is barely noticeable."

"There was a lot of pleasure…before."

"I took you too quickly. I should have eased you into it."

"Would that have helped?"

"Yes."

"Have lots of experience do you, in deflowering virgins?"

He moved so he was lying beside her, propped up on his elbow. "No, actually. I had never bedded a virgin before."

"Then how would you know?"

The look he gave her made her squirm inside.

"I am so not in your league, Tomasso," she whispered sadly.

He traced the lines of her face with one gentle fingertip. "In this you are wrong."

"I'm not."

"You are the woman I want to be the mother of my children…that puts you in my league." Then, before she could utter another protest, his mouth covered hers in a tender kiss.

She'd been expecting more claim-staking aggression when their lips met, but had no desire to halt this gentle onslaught. His lips moved over hers, teasing her to a response her body was only too happy to give. Within seconds she was all hot and quivery inside, her inner core pulsing with a desire that overwhelmed her.

His hands were everywhere, touching her, stroking her, exploring every inch of her exposed flesh and then trespassing the lines of her swimsuit to shock her with intimacies that made her moan.

"Shh…" he whispered in her ear. "The children."

Remembering, she tightened her throat on another moan and buried her fingers in his longish hair, gripping it tightly. He didn't complain, but kept up the kissing and touching until her body felt on fire with needs and desires only he had ever been able to create in her.

"Papa, why are you kissing Maggie?"

The sleepy child's voice barely dented her passionate stupor, but Tomasso pulled back with a cool ease that shamed her. He smiled at Anna, who had sat up and was rubbing her eyes. "I like to kiss Maggie."

Did his daughter believe that because he was her papa and a prince, that excuse was sufficient? If Tomasso Scorsolini liked doing something, he automatically got to do it, Maggie thought wildly. But she had liked it, too.

Much too much.

"Will you make her our mama then?" Anna asked.

"Perhaps."

Maggie was amazed that he did not come right out and say yes, considering his arrogant belief that she would fall in with his plans despite her protests.

She asked him about it later that night, after the children were in bed. She'd come into the lounge to read a book and he had been making phone calls in his study, but had joined her moments before.

He swirled the Scotch in his glass and looked at her.

"I will not make promises to my children I am not positive I can keep."

"I thought you were convinced you would get your own way."

"I cannot force you to marry me."

"But you are sure you can seduce me into it."

"It is only a matter of time before I have you in my bed again," he said without bothering to deny it.

"Has anyone ever told you that you're so primitive you belong in an exhibit on prehistoric man?"

"No. I am fairly certain I would remember such a comment."

"Well, I'm saying it."

"Wanting you does not make me a Neanderthal."

"Your belief you can drag me off by my hair does." And she didn't believe for a minute he wanted her. Not really. Men could manufacture desire, couldn't they?

All he had to do was think of someone else, someone more exciting, as he had the first time they'd almost made love. She was his answer to domestic harmony, not a woman he could love and passionately desire on her own merits.

"I have no desire to drag you anywhere. I wish for you to come to me willingly."

"You want me to engineer my own downfall?"

"Marriage to me is not a pit to fall into," he said with an expression she didn't understand. "I have no desire to jail you."

"I never said you did."

He visibly shook off whatever was bothering him. "Of course not."

"Did Liana accuse you of that?"

"The joys of living the life of royalty palled very quickly under the strictures it imposed."

"But surely she did not blame you for that."

"Yes, she did. Just as she blamed me when she became pregnant a second time."

"Didn't she want more children?"

"No."

"But…"

"She agreed to carry the baby to term if I would agree to allow her total personal freedom after Anna's birth."

"Oh, my gosh. I can't believe she did that."

He shrugged as if he had long ago come to terms with his wife's mercenary attitude toward her children. "She knew it was her best chance at getting what she wanted."

"Which was what?"

"The life of a princess without any of the responsibilities."

"But that's horribly selfish."

"Yes. And in the end, her selfishness killed her. She was parasailing in Mexico with a company that did not even have proper licensing when she was killed. She chose to go on the trip without me, without her children—she chose to dismiss her bodyguard's fervent request she not sail with that company. She had the freedom to do so, you see. I'd given it to her. And she died."

"You can't feel responsible!"

"Can't I? She was my wife and I did not protect her."

"She didn't want to be protected and from what I can tell, she didn't want to be a wife…not really."

"You are right. I will not make that mistake in marriage again."

"But not all beautiful women are that self-absorbed and spoiled."

"It does not matter. We are not talking about other women when it comes to marriage. We are talking about you only. For you alone are possibly pregnant with my child."

But once again, he had not denied that he did not find her beautiful. Oh, sure…he was attracted to her, but that wasn't the same thing as looking at her and being bowled over by her beauty. She'd seen him looking at Liana that way, and she would never forget it. He could never love an ordinary woman like Maggie and that was the most painful truth of all.

The next day, he informed her that she and the children would be accompanying him to Scorsolini Island for his father's birthday celebration the week after next.

"I'd prefer to take those two days as my days off."

"I want your help with the children."

"But you don't need me there, not with your sister-in-law on site. She's wonderful with the children."

"She's also in charge of the celebration events. She does not have the time to devote to my family, and why should she when I have you to help me care for Anna and Gianni?"

"You don't *have* me. I'm your nanny, and my contract stipulates at least one day off per week and all evenings when you are not away on business."

"You begrudge eating dinner with the children and me?"

She rolled her eyes at his obtuseness. "No."

"You do not wish to tuck them into bed at night?"

"That isn't the point."

"What is the point, Maggie?"

"I don't want to go to Scorsolini Island with you."

"Why not?"

Because she didn't want to see him around the beautiful women of his set, didn't want to witness him flirting with women who were far more suited to the role of princess than she was. "It's just not my scene."

"Are you telling me you never socialized with your employers and their children in your previous two positions?"

"Well, no…" In fact, they had always assumed she

would attend social functions to care for their children's needs so they could concentrate on the socializing aspect.

"Then this is no different."

"What day do you plan to give me off then?" she asked, stubbornly determined to gain some ground here.

He tensed as if he was really bothered by the question. "When you worked as my housekeeper you were content to be with me every day."

"That was then, this is now."

Looking inexplicably offended and definitely irritated, he said, "If you must have a day off, then make it the day before we leave for the other island."

"Thank you. And this week?"

"Do not thank me for merely doing my duty to fulfill our *business* contract. As for this week, take whatever day you like. You can inform my secretary of your decision so arrangements can be made for the children."

"Do you have business meetings over the weekend?"

"Not on Sunday. Do you want one of those days off?"

"Sunday would be fine."

"So be it," he said and turned to address Gianni about something.

She felt chilled by the dismissal, but she also wondered at it. Tomasso was a businessman to his toenails and yet he resented adherence to the business contract between them. It was another confusing puzzle in a long line of them where he was concerned.

He was still responding with cold politeness toward her two hours later when he received a phone call that made him frown and mutter something in Italian that got him a scolding from Anna.

"What is the matter?" she asked as he flipped his phone shut.

"You will get your wish to be rid of my presence earlier than anticipated. There is a problem with one of our lithium customers in China. Negotiations have hit a wall because of government requirements related to imported raw materials. I have to leave for Beijing tonight."

"But you just got back from a trip abroad. You told the children you would be home with them for at least another day."

He looked driven. "This cannot be helped."

"It's okay, Papa," Gianni said, his face set in stoic lines Maggie hated to see on a five-year-old.

"Why can't you take them with you?"

"That is not practical."

"Why not? If you're going to travel so much, you need to be prepared to take your family with you. It's not as if you can't afford the extra tickets."

"It is not a matter of tickets. I travel by private jet, but taking them would require taking you."

"Naturally."

"You do not mind this?"

"Why should I? As their nanny, my primary concern is the children's welfare."

"And you think it is best served by traveling with their papa?"

"Sometimes, yes."

"Do you like to travel?"

"Yes. I did quite a bit of it with the first family I worked for. I can have the children and myself packed within the hour."

"That was not in your file."

"My file?" she asked delicately.

"What's a file?" Gianni asked, when the silence between the adults had stretched uncomfortably.

"In this case, I believe it refers to a report compiled about a person. Me. Is that right?" she asked Tomasso.

"Yes. It is so."

"What kind of report?" Anna asked.

"An investigative report," Tomasso answered flatly.

"You had me investigated?" She should have known he didn't trust her—he'd doubted her after that first night—but it still hurt.

"Naturally. All Scorsolini employees have background checks run on them."

And that said everything about how he saw her position as his wife if she were to marry him.

"I see."

The provoking little witch, Tomasso thought.

He didn't know what it was she thought she saw, but from the expression in her usually warm gray eyes, it wasn't something that put him in a complimentary light. The last two days had shown him that she was a perfect fit with him and his children. However, she stubbornly refused to acknowledge it.

But she wanted him. No matter how she tried to disguise it, her face and trembling body gave her away. However, she was adept at escaping to her suite or hiding behind the children's presence to keep him at bay. He allowed it because he wanted her to come to him of her own free will, but perhaps he was playing the game the wrong way.

He wanted her to be his wife. His instincts had been right from the beginning. She was everything he remembered and their shared passion was perfect. He would have no problem maintaining fidelity in the marriage bed, but he would not make the mistake this time of confusing lust with love.

He liked Maggie and that was more than he had felt for Liana at the end.

Though he had to admit, to himself only, that it would not bother him if she fancied herself in love with him again. It would make her happier because she wanted to marry for love, and he wanted her to be happy. He however, did not need to believe himself in love to be content with the prospect of marriage to her...particularly if she were pregnant with his child.

This trip to China could turn out to be a smart tactical move on his part, as well as a welcome opportunity to keep his children with him. Sharing a single hotel suite, even one with three bedrooms, would force them into a proximity she had avoided.

True to her word, Maggie and the children were ready to leave for Tomasso's private airstrip exactly one hour later.

She carried a large duffle bag onto the plane with her and when he asked about it, she smiled. "It's filled with their favorite games, art supplies and snacks. I wasn't at all sure your private jet would be stocked with the kind of snacks children like to eat while traveling."

"No doubt you are right. We usually take the yacht when we travel to one of the other islands."

"They never travel with you anywhere else?"

"To Italy to visit my stepmother, but then my staff know to prepare the plane for the children's presence and we usually do our journeying at night so they sleep for most of the trip."

"Your stepmother?"

For some reason it surprised him that she did not know about Flavia. "My father remarried within a year of my mother's death."

"The Queen of Isole dei Re lives in Italy?"

"She is no longer the queen. She divorced him when Marcello was small."

Maggie's face registered almost comical shock. "Why?"

"My father had an affair. She refused to forgive him."

"How horrible for her, but I'm surprised she divorced him for such a thing. I thought royal marriages lasted no matter what."

"She preferred life without a crown if it meant separation from a philandering husband." And he had respected her for it.

"Wow."

"You sound as if you admire her."

"I do. That must have taken a lot of courage. Did your father fight for custody?"

"Not that I am aware of. He even allowed Claudio and me to stay with her weeks at a time on several occasions each year."

"How unusual."

"Not really. He was hardly in a position to raise three sons without the help of a wife, and she had become our mother for all intents and purposes."

"I guess as king, he was too busy to be a single parent."

"Yes. I have never envied my brother his claim to the throne."

"I can understand that, but I always had the impression you were trying to prove something."

"That I could make it in life without my position? I used to feel that way." He'd given up worrying about it after learning Liana had known he was royalty when they met.

"You succeeded."

"To an extent."

"Your father never married again."

"No. He chose a string of mistresses over compromising his own sense of honor by speaking vows he did not think he would keep."

"Why wouldn't he keep them?"

"The Scorsolini Curse…or so he says."

"What in the world is that?"

"According to my father, the men in the Scorsolini family are fated to love once and to love so deeply that if the true love is lost then there is no chance another woman could ever take her place."

"That's an ingenious excuse for serial adultery."

"Not adultery. I told you, he did not remarry."

"But he assumed he would commit adultery if he did."

"Yes."

Maggie eyed him askance, her gray depths speaking messages he had not trouble interpreting. "Are you similarly inclined?"

"No. I do not break my promises."

"So you don't buy your dad's excuse?"

"No. Actually I don't."

"I would like to meet your stepmother, I think."

"I will arrange it. You will like her. She is very down to earth and warm. She gave my brothers and I a sense of family and normalcy in our childhood despite the fact we were princes. She is the only person who dares to scold Claudio, even now."

"She sounds wonderful."

"She is. You remind me of her in many ways." Suddenly he realized that one of his main reasons for seeking Maggie out was how similar she was to Flavia.

He knew he could trust Flavia and felt the same way about Maggie. He'd doubted her at first, but now that he understood how she'd come to allow him to make love to her, he accepted she was the same woman of integrity he had known six years ago.

CHAPTER EIGHT

THE first leg of the flight went surprisingly well. While Gianni and Anna were younger than her previous charges, Maggie had a lot of experience keeping children occupied on long journeys. Besides, it was much more comfortable on Tomasso's private jet than it ever had been on a commercial flight, even in first class. He had to work for several hours of the first leg, but put his papers aside to eat lunch with her and the children.

He turned his focus entirely on them—and her—while they ate, making the children beam and unnerving her.

For a workaholic, he had a surprising ability to set his work aside.

When they stopped to refuel, he surprised Maggie by leading them off the plane. He took them all to eat at a local restaurant for dinner and then arranged to go to an outdoor play area for the children he'd had his staff locate.

"Don't we have to get back in the air?" she asked as Gianni and Anna ran toward the merry-go-round.

"We will have a much more pleasant second half of our journey if we allow the children to use up their excess energy so they will sleep."

"The first half wasn't so bad."

"It was not bad at all. You did an excellent job with them. I was very impressed, but it is late and if we do not give them time to play, they will spend the rest of the flight fretting instead of sleeping."

"You know your children very well, don't you?"

"Naturally."

"You're a good father. I'm sorry Liana wasn't more interested in family life. If she had been, you would have made an excellent team."

"I am counting on that team being you and I, Maggie."

"It's not the same."

"Are you saying it would bother you to be the mother for two children to whom you had not given birth?"

Anna sat on the merry-go-round while Gianni pushed it and then jumped on, both of them shrieking with laughter as it whirled. They were both so precious...so loveable.

"That's not the problem. How could it be?"

"Liana did not wish to be a mother to her own children. Many women would hesitate to take on that role with children that are not their own."

"I'm not those other women, nor am I Liana." In more ways than one, she thought. But in this instance, she certainly didn't mind. "And I don't believe you would have any trouble finding a stadium full of women who would willingly be stepmother to your children if it meant a chance to marry you and wear that princess crown you were so sure I wanted to trade my virginity for."

His gaze settled on her, all serious and intent. "I have admitted I was wrong, have I not?"

"Yes, but you never said you were sorry for thinking it in the first place." Which bothered her. She'd never give him reason to believe badly of her.

"And you believe I should?"

"Absolutely." She turned to face him, leaving the children's safety to the security team hovering at a discreet distance. "Your cynicism is no excuse for insulting my honor."

His blue eyes sparkled with latent humor. "I am deeply remorseful and beg your pardon most humbly."

"You're laughing at me."

He smiled and it was like an arrow straight to her heart. "Perhaps a little but I am sincerely sorry for offending you. You are much too innocent to have hatched such a scheme."

"Honest. I'm much too *honest*."

"That, too."

She nodded with satisfaction, though his belief she was so innocent rankled a little. It was akin to him thinking she was too dumb to have hatched such a plan. She wasn't, she simply had too much integrity to allow her mind to go sailing in such murky waters.

He brushed a curling strand of hair from her face, leaving a path of aroused nerve endings in the wake of his touch. "So, what is the problem?"

"Problem?" What was he talking about?

"You said the children were not the reason you are balking at marriage to me. That still leaves some obstacle in your mind to be overcome."

"There is the little matter of love between us, or lack thereof." And the fact that no matter how much she might come to love him, he could never, ever love her.

She wasn't princess material and never would be. She wasn't beautiful, she wasn't sophisticated and a regal bearing would really be beyond her. Wouldn't he always be comparing her to that kind of woman and finding her wanting? Part of her wished she could be those things for him. That she could somehow earn his love like she'd earned her place in the foster homes she'd lived in.

But an even bigger part of her wished she didn't have to, wished that his proposal had been sparked by love and not convenience, and that he wanted her heart for the future, not just a glorified nanny and bed warmer.

She'd spent her whole life earning her place through work and the thought of being married for the same reason was really painful. Millions of women just as ordinary as she was were loved by the men that had captured their hearts…why did she have to have gotten involved with a blasted prince?

"Did you know that a socially accepted view of love as the basis of marriage did not come into being until 1200 AD?"

It was not a welcome question on the heels of her thoughts. "Well, it's in existence now."

"Even then, not every culture adopted it," he continued as if she had said nothing. "And among the ruling class it took much, much longer to take root, even in the Western world. My own family did not have their first marriage for love until 1809 and it was 1866 before the first Scorsolini king married a woman of his choice rather than arranging an advantageous political match."

"I don't know what you think that has to do with me."

"Family history is filled with accounts of successful and by all accounts, happy marriages."

"And some not so happy. I don't want to play out the scenario your father played with Flavia."

"I have told you, I do not break my promises. I was faithful to Liana for the entire four years of our marriage, never even looking at another woman with intent."

"I believe you."

"So why are you so worried?"

"Liana was gorgeous and sophisticated. While she obviously failed in the mothering stakes, she was the ideal companion for you."

"You think so?"

"Obviously. She was everything any prince could want. She was beautiful and sexy. You used to watch her with a look of total enthrallment. She was passionately full of life and that charmed you. I remember."

"She was filled with passion for the pleasures of life. That is not the same thing, as I learned too late. And none of the other things you mention made up for her selfish disregard of our children's feelings and needs. Believe me. Beauty that is only skin deep pales quickly."

So he said, but that beauty had been enough to catch his attention completely, enough to make him forget the paltry attraction he had had toward Maggie. And no matter what he said, it must have kept his interest because he'd remained with her despite her incredible shortcomings as a mother. Family was obviously important to him, so to her mind it was very telling he had stayed with Liana even after she blackmailed him with her pregnancy.

"You stayed married to her," Maggie said almost accusingly.

"And remained faithful," he replied grimly.

"Why?"

"She was my wife. I made the mistake, I would not divorce her and hurt the children further. At least as my wife, she saw them more frequently than she would have as my ex."

"The fact you were very attracted to her had to have helped."

"The passion I felt toward Liana had burned out by the third year of our marriage."

Far from making Maggie feel more confident, that knowledge seared her to her soul. If he had stopped wanting a woman like Liana, how could she hope to maintain his sexual interest for a lifetime?

"I notice you do not ask why."

"I would say it was obvious. She no longer appealed to you."

"No, she did not, but not for the reason you seem to believe. I did not turn my eye to another woman."

"Then what?"

"I could not feel strong desire for a woman who used her pregnancy as a bargaining chip and then later pursued her own pleasures while ignoring our children."

"Yet you continued to make love to her."

"I am a man. I have needs and they had to be met in the marriage bed."

The picture he painted of his marriage was a chilling one.

"I could not stand being married to a man who did not want me."

"That will not happen."

"How can you say that after what you just told me?"

He sighed in exasperation. "Don't you hear anything I say? What draws me to you is not something that can ever change."

"What do you mean?"

"I desire your delectable body, but it is the character inside you that acts like a continuous aphrodisiac to my senses."

"Yeah, right," she said indelicately…though *her* senses were busy trying to deal with the arousing nature of his nearness. But delectable body? Could he really think that?

"I am not making a joke here. Your generous spirit is not only a total sexual turn-on, but it is addictive. I want you, Maggie."

"You keep saying that."

"Because it is true. And I will have you."

He'd said that more than once, too. "Not here. Not now," she couldn't resist saying.

"Soon."

The promise in his voice and eyes made her shiver and in self-defense, she turned away to watch the children again.

She couldn't turn away from his claim that it was her character he found so inspiring, though. She found it inconceivable and wasn't sure she believed him, but as cynical as he was, she'd never known him to lie. Was it possible that, despite the fact she wasn't beautiful and he most likely would never love her, she could hold his sexual interest in marriage and friendship? Just by being herself?

And if she did enter such a one-sided marriage, loving him and not being truly loved in return...would that really be enough for her?

By the time they left the play area, Gianni and Anna were so tired, they were both drooping. When they got back to the plane, Maggie went to pull back the covers on the bed in the small bedroom when Tomasso stopped her. "The children can sleep comfortably on the reclined seats because they are so small. You will use the bed."

"But—"

"Do not argue with me. Do you not realize I'm the prince around here?"

"You're bossy, is what you are." She smiled. "At least I understand how you got that way now."

"And how is that?"

"You got used to giving orders, being royalty and all. I can't believe I never knew you were a prince six years ago. You were always uncannily regal in your bearing."

He laughed, but sobered when she did not smile or laugh in response. "What is it?"

"You said you thought you were my friend back then."

"We were friends, though you tried to deny it once."

It hadn't done her any good. Walking away from him had not meant forgetting. She had missed him, both his friendship and what might have been. Her dreams had kept the feelings alive and no other man had ever impinged on that part of her heart.

"I admit it now."

"Good."

"But if we *were* friends, why didn't you ever tell me of your true identity? You didn't trust me," she added, answering her own question.

He sighed. "I wanted to be accepted for who I was, not what I was."

"But I'd already accepted you."

"Did you? You walked away from me and our so-called friendship. Would you find that so easy to do now?"

"What do you mean *now?* Because we, um…" She let her voice trail off, not wanting to say what she was thinking with two sleepy children as witnesses.

"Because now you know I am a prince."

She rolled her eyes. "Don't be stupid. Your being a prince has nothing to do with it."

"Perhaps." But she could tell he didn't believe her.

That bothered her the whole time she and Tomasso readied the children for bed and got them snuggled into their reclined seats with blankets and comfy down pillows.

He was vulnerable to his position. The thought shocked her, but when she considered some things he had said and how hard he had worked to prove himself not only in college, but since, building a new industry for Isole dei Re, she realized it was true. And she hated knowing that he believed she was like so many others in valuing him because of his position and not who he was.

If she told him the truth about six years ago, she could dispel those beliefs, but it would mean admitting to feelings that had not been returned.

She'd protected herself once. For the sake of her pride and emotions, she had abandoned their friendship. She had hurt him and unwittingly fed his belief he could not be cared for simply as a man, as opposed to the man who wore the crown.

For reasons she did not want to analyze too closely, she could not stand for him to continue to labor under that misapprehension on her account.

"Your whole life has been both blessed and marked by your status as a prince, hasn't it?" she asked as he pulled her into a seat beside where he had been working before they'd landed for refueling.

He shrugged and that shrug did things to her heart that she didn't want to acknowledge in this lifetime. It said that as cool as he appeared, she had touched something raw inside him.

"I walked away from our friendship six years ago because it hurt too much to see you and Liana together. I loved you and it devastated me that you were so obviously in love with her. It had nothing to do with your status, or lack thereof. I can guarantee you that knowing you were a prince would only have solidified my decision. Being around the two of you made me realize how hopeless my feelings for you were. It would only have been worse, knowing you were royalty."

He frowned. "I hurt you very much that night I came home with Liana, didn't I?"

She didn't want to talk about that night. The memories were too sharp no matter how much she'd tried to forget. "You came home with Liana on lots of nights, and yes…it hurt. I didn't want to walk away from you—that hurt, too, but not as much as it would have watching the two of you together."

"I am sorry about that night."

"You said so at the time, and I didn't bring this up to dredge another apology out of you. I just wanted you to know it wasn't about you being a prince."

"I find it curious that, though I hurt you six years ago and you've made it clear you find my current proposal more an insult, you still care enough to try to protect my feelings. Most people would say I don't have any feelings to protect."

"They would be wrong."

His expression mocked her and she let out an exasperated breath. "Just call me a pushover then. I care too much about other people's feelings for my own good."

"You are not a pushover, but a rarity in this world: a woman who cares deeply for others."

"I'm not so rare. You just move in the wrong circles."

"Perhaps." His gaze snagged hers and held on. "I have regretted many times my timing in meeting Liana."

She never had. If he'd met the beautiful woman after they had slept together, Maggie's pain would have been multiplied tenfold because she had absolutely no doubt the outcome would have been the same. He would have ended up with Liana and she would have ended up alone.

"It was for the best," was all she said now as she broke eye contact and grabbed a magazine to skim.

Tomasso watched Maggie close the door on the bedroom, frustration roiling through him.

Didn't all the pop psychologists say that talking was supposed to bring two people closer together? But every time he and Maggie talked, she pulled further away from him. He had thought admitting that he had regretted falling for Liana and leaving Maggie untouched six years ago would make her see that she belonged with him.

Instead she'd made it clear that she did not think him turning to Liana instead of her was that great a tragedy.

Was that because she had found it so easy to dismiss her love for him? He had very little confidence in the emotion. His father said he had loved Tomasso's mother, but had certainly never loved any of the women who had shared his life since, including Flavia.

Claudio and Therese had a peaceful marriage, the kind Tomasso desired, but he had seen no evidence that his brother was crazily in love. Marcello had loved his wife, but she had died too soon for that emotion to be tested by time or adverse circumstance.

Tomasso personally believed that the emotion was an excuse strong men employed to justify weakness and to follow the impulses of passion rather than duty.

He had seen it too many times amidst the people of his world who used love as an excuse for infidelity and even the abandonment of responsibility to one's children or country. So why did the thought that Maggie no longer loved him annoy him?

Because there was no denying it did. Every time she said it, or implied that was the case, he was filled with an inexplicable anger and desire to make her recant her words.

No doubt it was for the sake of his children and his own peace of mind. He wanted her tied to him with unbreakable bonds. He did not have to trust in the emotion to know that if Maggie thought herself in love, she would be committed to him, body and soul. In a way Liana had never been.

Maggie would be his.

As she was meant to be.

Maggie snuggled into the heat surrounding her, a familiar scent from her dreams filling her with a sense of blissful peace. A warm weight that did not feel like a blanket shifted on her hip, sliding down her thigh. Her sense of drowsiness dissipated as her mind grew cognizant of the fact she was not alone.

Her eyes flicked open and in the dim blue glow given off by the emergency lighting beside the door she saw Tomasso. He faced her, his eyes closed, his breathing even and shallow.

He was asleep.

In her bed.

He was also dressed, or at least sort of. He wore a pair of shorts and a T-shirt, not an outfit she'd ever seen him in. Even on the beach, where he wore swim trunks that showed off his sculpted body to perfection or a polo shirt and tailored shorts. A curl of midnight-black hair fell over his forehead endearingly and she had to stifle the urge to reach up and smooth it back. She did not want to wake him.

No doubt he'd decided that sharing the bed made more sense than him trying to sleep in a reclining seat, but he had not gotten beneath the covers with her. She appreciated that. It showed that no matter how possessively he spoke to her, he respected her right to choose how far she was willing to go in this relationship.

It also indicated that, regardless of the fiasco of his first night home, he did not consider he had the right to climb naked into a bed with her in it. Not when he was in full possession of his reasoning anyway. In retrospect, if the consequences of that night had not been so serious, the fact he'd talked himself into doing so because of his inebriated (or close to it) state was almost kind of funny.

It was just so out of character. He'd blown his own plan because he'd been thinking fuzzy, and for some strange reason she couldn't begin to decipher, she found that endearing.

That thought made her smile.

In more ways than one, he'd tempered his arrogance for her. Though he certainly had not relinquished it completely. He *was* still in her bed, after all.

"You are smiling," he rumbled in a sleep-husky voice. His eyes, which she had not appreciated were now slit, opened fully. "You like waking beside me?"

She shook her head in disbelief at her own naiveté. "And I thought your arrogance was tempered."

"Why would you want it tempered?" he asked lazily. "You like me as I am."

"Do you always wake with these conceited delusions?"

"Is it conceited to believe it is not only my children's company you find pleasant?" The question sounded serious rather than teasing.

"I decline to answer that question on the grounds it could incriminate me."

"Aha!" He rolled in a swift move that took her by surprise and ended with her under him. "All of this nonsense about you having your days off was on principle, not desire, was it not?"

The blanket pinned her so she could not move, which worried her less than the fact her body was reacting to his position over her in a predictable and very uncomfortable fashion.

CHAPTER NINE

"HAVING regular days off is not nonsense," she argued in an attempt to hide the uncontrollable response from him.

But she was afraid it was a losing battle. Desire was part of love and she loved this man more than anything or anyone else in the world. She'd finally admitted that to herself when she'd come to bed. She'd known he still had a special place in her heart, but after talking to him and admitting her love from six years ago and seeing how affected he was by being wanted only for his status...well, her heart had just cracked wide-open.

She'd gone to sleep with the knowledge that she would love this man to her grave pumping in her heart.

"In our case, it is."

"You don't own me, Tomasso. Even royalty aren't allowed to keep slaves anymore."

He looked seriously offended. "Slavery has never been legal in Isole dei Re and I have no wish to make you my slave."

"Then why begrudge me time off?"

"I do not begrudge it. Surely you know that if you need time to do things for yourself, I will make certain you have it."

"Then why complain about my regular time off?"

"Because you would spend unnecessary time away from me and the children." He wanted to marry her to make his life easier, not harder. Somehow, he knew things would be harder when she wasn't there.

She sighed. "And if one of the things I want to do for myself is something as simple as taking a long bath and reading a book? How necessary would you see that being?"

"As imperative as you want me to. I would make certain you have the time to do so, though I can think of things much more interesting to do in the bath than to read."

"I'm sure you could, but as we've already discussed, I'm not up to your speed."

"In what way?"

"Too many to count, but I'm not exactly princess material, Tomasso."

"According to who?"

"Me."

"You have no experience in such matters and will therefore have to trust me when I tell you that you are wrong. You would make an ideal Scorsolini princess."

"You've got to be kidding."

"I am not. It comes back to character again—you have both the character and integrity for the job."

"I never considered getting married as a job." But then, for most children, being the daughter in a household wasn't a job, either. It had been for her, though.

She'd had to work to earn her place, and now he wanted her to work to earn her place as his wife.

"In many ways, that is exactly what it is." He put his hand over her mouth when she opened it to speak. "And that is not a bad thing. Marriage comes with a defined set of expectations that when fulfilled benefit both parties."

She turned her head so his hand no longer covered her

mouth. "You make it sound just like a business proposition when it should be so much more."

"It is more."

And she knew exactly what he was talking about. Sex. That wasn't enough, but it was all he was offering. Why did it have to hurt so much? If she were mercenary, she'd take his offer and run with it all the way to a really beneficial prenuptial contract. "I told you, I'm not up to your speed in that way."

"In what way?"

"The sex thing." As if he really didn't know.

"I could take you there," he said with a sensual smile.

And end up breaking her heart in the process...not that it felt all that whole anymore regardless. Loving another person hurt. For her, that was all it seemed to do. She'd loved her parents and losing them had shattered her child's heart. She'd loved a foster mom who saw her as nothing more than a source of income and free labor, and she'd loved him.

Her feelings six years ago had given her no joy and a lot of pain. Now she loved both him and his children and knew that to stay would hurt, but so would walking away. Much more than she had hurt six years ago.

Life wasn't fair and she knew that, but sometimes it felt like she was destined for more pain than she could deal with.

"No thank you." And even as she said the words, she wasn't sure she meant them.

She did love him and she wanted him desperately. It didn't seem to matter that she'd been hurt by him the two times she'd thought to make love with him...her heart wanted to try one more time to find an emotional connection through a physical conduit. Her brain screamed that it hadn't worked before and it wouldn't work this time, but her heart wasn't listening.

It beat with incessant hope that she didn't understand, but could not ignore, either.

That foolish organ insisted that things were different now. That Tomasso wanted more from her than he'd wanted before, that if all she could have from him was physical love, it was better than no love at all. It reminded her that she was tired of being alone and he was promising her a future of togetherness, no matter how pragmatic his reasons for doing so.

"I think it is time I showed you how truly well we fit together," he said, showing he wasn't convinced by her denial either.

"I don't want to be used." Where the words came from, she wasn't sure. They hadn't been in her brain, or her heart, that she knew about, but they expressed her feelings very well.

He frowned down at her. "I have made my intentions clear. I want to marry you, Maggie. That is not using you."

"You think I'm pregnant. If you didn't, you'd still be deciding if I was suitable wife material or not." And her susceptible heart would be smart to remember that.

"Even if we had not made love that first night, I would have realized very quickly how well you fit with my children and myself."

She shook her head, not wanting to believe him because if she did, her defenses were going to crumble.

"Yes. You are the woman we need to make our family complete."

"You don't love me, Tomasso."

"So?" he asked as if the single word, confirming his lack of feelings was not like a knife slashing right through her heart.

"*So?*" she repeated in a near whisper.

"Love is not a requirement for a happy marriage. I will be faithful. I will take care of you. You will have my respect, my consideration and God willing, we will have more children together. What more could a man who loves you give you?"

"His heart."

"You will have my loyalty, my commitment and my honor. It is enough."

"Your arrogance is showing again."

"Because I know what is right for me?"

"Because you are so sure you know what is right for *me*."

"But I do know this."

"You're only thinking about what is best for you and trying to convince me that it is what is best for me too."

"You are wrong. I care very much about what is best for you, but consider, Maggie…you are twenty-six years old. Until three nights ago, you were a virgin. You had not had a single serious relationship with a man."

"Did your report tell you that?"

"Yes. It also told me that you are a loner, but your heart is too generous to be comfortable in a lonely existence."

"Being a loner does not mean I was lonely."

"But you were. Admit it, for it is the truth."

He was right. There was a kind of loneliness that came from not having any family that people with a family could never understand. She had no one, and had had no one since she was eight years old. "So what?" she said, despite his perception of her pain. "We can't all have big families and oodles of friends. My job dictated that most of my time was spent with children, not adults."

"If you married me, you would become part of my family. My papa would be your papa, Flavia would care for you like a beloved daughter just as she does Therese, my children would be your children, my friends would be your friends. You would have *me*."

"Conceited." But, oh gosh…his words were more seductive than his body, and that was saying something.

"Practical. We were friends once. There is no reason we cannot share that friendship again. I know I would enjoy it, but just as important, you need it. You need *me*…even if you are too stubborn to admit it."

"It's not stubbornness."

"What is it then?"

"Fear," she answered baldly with more honesty than she had planned, and immediately wished the single word unsaid.

"What do you fear?"

"Having a family and then losing it again." The words came from a place inside her she thought she'd dealt with a long time ago.

"Like you lost your parents."

"And my foster care families. Permanent ties just don't work in my life."

"I will make them work."

"How can you?"

"I have told you. I will never let you go…and I will never leave you."

"That's easy to say now, but even you can't promise that."

"You mean death, do you not?"

"Yes."

"Everyone dies, Maggie, but to pull away from committing to the living because of it is to live a very lonely existence."

"Maybe lonely is better than hurting." Only it hurt, too, always being alone. It hurt so much.

"It is not."

"You're always so darn sure of yourself."

"It is my job to be sure."

"For your companies maybe, but not for other people."

"For you. Maggie, you are mine and one day soon you will realize it."

She glared at him. "Stop saying that."

"Stop denying it."

The whole time they'd been talking, he'd been on top of her, his body calling to hers, his nearness causing all sorts of reactions in her. The biggest one in her heart, but she felt an empty ache in her most feminine place, too. And her nipples stung against the soft cotton of her nightie. He hadn't touched her, but her breasts were swollen and craving the feel of his fingers and her thighs shifted in an invitation as old as time, as natural as it was risky.

She wanted to kiss him, to taste his mouth on hers and the salty maleness of his skin. She wanted to be naked with him and he with her like they had been that night. But this time she would touch him and concentrate intently on how it felt to be touched….not like in a dream, but for real. Because despite the discomfort of losing her virginity, the other night still had a dreamlike quality for her.

She wanted a taste of reality. Tonight she didn't want to worry about the future, or whether or not a relationship would work between them. For right now, she wanted to be exactly what he claimed she was…his woman.

And she wanted to try this one last time to fill the void in her heart with physical love. Emotional love was not on offer in her life, but this was, and the debacle of the other night could not obliterate the hope that burned too deeply to be quenched by mere logic or her brain's warnings.

"Maggie?"

"What?" she forced out of a throat dry with desire.

"Tell me what you want."

"I thought you knew."

"I need to hear the words."

"You're so sure of what they'll be?"

"I am."

But still he wanted the words. Maybe he wasn't as certain as he wanted her to believe. Or he simply wanted her to be aware of her choice. She'd accused him of taking advantage before, but he hadn't. Not on purpose. He shouldn't have gotten into bed with her that first time, but she believed he had done it without the intent to seduce. Her reaction to his kiss had been the downfall for both of them…something he could never have predicted and neither could she.

But now he wanted her cognizant agreement and she was ready to give it. She didn't want to hold back any longer. Not tonight. She was feeling much too vulnerable in her rediscovered love. She needed this. She needed him.

"I want you, Tomasso."

His big body shuddered and he was silent for a long moment. "Are you sure?"

"Yes."

He kissed her then, a soft claiming of her lips that left her wanting more when he broke his lips from hers and stood. He pulled off his clothes in the dim blue light as naturally as if he'd been stripping naked for her every day for the past six years. His gaze caught hers as he skimmed his shorts down his hair-roughened masculine thighs. She couldn't help looking at what he had revealed, her gaze drawn as powerfully as if controlled by an outside force. And it was…his overt sexiness. He was so incredibly attractive. Every part of him.

Daunting, too. He was so very much a man.

Her eyes felt like they were bugging out of her head as she fixed them on his arousal. "Is that normal?" she croaked. "No wonder it hurt."

But did she want to change her mind? No. Which said a lot for the power of desire.

He choked on a laugh and shook his head. "I assure you, I am no monster, but you are very innocent." His eyes burned with satisfaction, their blue depths so dark they looked like a reflection of the night sky. "I find that much more exciting than I should. I am, after all, a liberated man."

It was her turn to laugh despite her nervousness. "Liberated for the Stone Age, maybe."

"You think I am a throwback?"

"You believe you have to marry me because I was a virgin the first time we made love and I might be pregnant. You think I *belong* to you for those same reasons. Yes, I would say that puts you in the running for Neanderthal Man of the Year."

He stilled, his regard intent. "And this bothers you?"

Remembering what he had shared about Liana's accusations that living with him was like being in a prison, Maggie stifled her inclination to give him a flippant retort. "Honestly?" she asked.

"*Sì*. Always, I want honesty from you."

"And will you give it?"

"Always. No lies. Ever."

That was pretty conclusive and the promise sent a sense of warm pleasure deep into her heart. "Neanderthal Man has his charms."

He smiled, white teeth flashing. "I'm glad to hear it."

He walked toward her, his hard flesh not the only thing that drew her attention. Naked, this man was magnificent. Every muscle in his body was defined without making him look like a Mr Atlas wannabe and his tanned skin glowed even in the dim light.

"You're yummy, you know that?"

"The feeling is entirely mutual."

She bit her lip, knowing that it had to be his libido talking. She was too unremarkable to be considered delicious by this man, but she knew he meant the compliment when he said it, however unlikely. He did want her. The evidence was staring her in the face.

"Will you allow me to make love to you without the blankets, or do you wish to hide beneath them?"

She *was* hiding, her body covered from neck to toe by the light cotton blankets and sheet. She didn't want to hide from him. For her answer, she pushed the blankets aside to reveal a short gown of pale pink. There was nothing overtly sexy about it, but it stopped mid thigh and its thin material did nothing to hide the turgid state of her nipples. The flare of his eyes told her he noticed, too.

He ran a fingertip from the rapid pulse in her neck down over the curve of her breast and then circled one hard tip before brushing directly over it. She gasped, her hands clenching at her sides.

"You are so responsive." He traced his fingertip across her chest to her other breast, giving the same tortuous caresses to it. "You excite me until I ache."

"I ache, too," she whispered.

"Then I must assuage that ache."

"Yes…"

He came down beside her, his sex touching her thigh and she sucked in a shocked breath. The intimacy was so new. His member was warm and hard, but felt smooth against her, too. So different than what she would have expected and yet so wonderful too.

He laid his hand on her shoulder, brushing her collarbone with his thumb, his eyes devouring her like a hungry lion. "You have nothing to fear. I will not hurt you again."

Despite the voracious look, she believed him. She was hungry for him, too. "I'm not afraid."

"You are very tense."

She smiled, her heart beat going a mile a minute. "This is all new to me."

"I could tell."

She turned her head away, stung at what she took as a reminder of the disparity in their experience. "Don't make fun of me."

"I am not. I told you…" He kissed along her jaw. "Your innocence excites me." His lips played with the corner of hers, his tongue darting out to taste her in a way that made her shiver. "Very much."

Forcing away her fears of inadequacy, she turned and gave him her mouth. She held nothing back and the kiss turned carnal, its heat scorching her nerve endings into blazing life.

He touched her while their lips were locked in the sensual battle toward pleasure. His hands laid claim to every inch of her flesh, showing her that she had erogenous zones she would never have suspected existed. She touched him, too, exploring every part of his nakedness she could reach. He thrust against her when she touched his backside, but when her fingers curled tentatively around his member, he went completely and utterly still, breaking the kiss.

"Yes, touch me there, Maggie."

She caressed him up and down and he groaned against her lips, kissing her again with rapacious desire.

He let her explore, guiding her hand when she grew shy and showing her what he liked touched and how to do it in a way that made his body rigid with vibrating tension.

He pulled her hand away. "That is enough," he growled.

"But I like touching you."

"I like it, too, *tesoro mio,* but if you wish me to leave you insensate with pleasure, you must not push me too hard this first time."

"It isn't our first time."

"Thank the good God. We have no virgin barrier to deal with."

He gave her no chance to respond, but started touching her again, first through her nightgown and then removing it so he could caress her naked body. He knew exactly how and where to concentrate his caresses and soon, she was quivering with need. But he was far from done. He used his mouth to cover the same ground he had recently traversed with his hands.

She shook with pleasure upon pleasure as his lips and tongue made love to her in a way she had never dreamed.

When he kissed her inner thigh, using his teeth to bite gently and then snaking his tongue out to lick her sensitized flesh, she cried out.

His head came up. "You must not be noisy, sweet Maggie. We do not want the children to hear. This room is semisoundproofed, but I would not like to test its boundaries with them in the outer cabin."

"You mean you haven't had noisy lovers in here before?"

"I have never made love in here."

"Oh." She liked knowing that, though why it should matter she had no idea.

After all, she knew he was experienced, but she had a deep inner need she did not understand for this time to be unique and special…for both of them.

His head lowered between her legs again, the sight unbearably erotic to her. This time his tongue touched a spot far more sensitive than her inner thigh and she had to bite her lip to keep from screaming. She whimpered as he made love to her with his tongue, using his fingers to press inside her, stretching her tight and swollen tissues.

Then he took her sweet spot between his teeth and thrashed the hard little nub with the tip of his tongue over and over again.

She came apart, biting her hand to stop a shout of agonized pleasure from escaping as she repeatedly convulsed under his ministering tongue. She was trembling with the edgy aftershocks of pleasure when he swarmed up her body. He pressed the tip of his erection to her quivering entrance.

"You are ready?" he asked in a strained voice.

"Yes." She needed to feel him inside of her.

He entered her in a slow glide that teased her with what would come while he filled her completely. Unbelievably, as exhausted as she was, she began to move under him, needing more than the tantalizing slowness of this tender possession.

He was not slow to take the hint, and with a dark chuckle of triumph, he set a pace that soon had her writhing in renewed preorgasmic bliss.

"That's right, *tesoro*....move with me. Give me your passion, *bella*."

"Bella?" The humiliation crashed down on her. Not now, please, he couldn't be thinking of another woman now...

"Beautiful," he was saying. "You are so beautiful in your passion."

Beautiful? It was Italian. *Of course.*

The realization that all those years ago he hadn't been thinking of another woman got lost in her second climax. His mouth slammed over hers and he swallowed the scream she could not stifle. He went rigid above her, his arms tightening around her with passionate force as he found his completion inside her.

He collapsed. The weight of his big body should have been uncomfortable, but instead it felt right. Wonderful, in fact.

He nuzzled her neck. "You are an incredible lover."

"You're not so bad yourself."

"Naturally not."

She laughed at his arrogance, too sated with pleasure to take issue with his egotistical statement.

He lifted his head and shoulders, balancing on his forearms. "What we have here is very special. You have no other experience to compare it to, but you must believe me when I tell you few lovers reach such heights."

"What about you and Liana?" she asked before thinking and then wished she could bite out her own tongue.

But he did not look offended by her question, more thoughtful. "She always wanted to be seduced. She never gave of her passion freely, like you do. You are so generous with your womanly desire. You cannot know what a treasure that is." He kissed her. "Making love to you is unique and very, very *good*."

The lavish praise filled her with pleasure.

"It was better this time," she felt she should tell him.

The whispered confession made him laugh out loud. "I am glad. I did not like you thinking my lovemaking was not all that it should be."

It was her turn to giggle. "Don't tell me you were bothered by such a little thing."

"It is not little for a man to appear deficient in the eyes of his woman."

"You could never seem less in my eyes," she admitted to him, too thrown by what she'd just been through to protect her words. "You are everything I ever thought a man should be, Tomasso."

He smiled, looking really pleased. "Then you will agree to marry me."

"I—" But her words were cut off by lips making new and passionate demands upon her.

When Maggie woke, she was alone in the bed and wearing the T-shirt Tomasso had worn the night before. He must have slipped it on her while she slept because she didn't remember putting it on. She remembered making love… more than once. She remembered getting every bit as insensate with pleasure as he'd promised her she would. And she remembered his certainty that she would now marry him after the first time.

She wasn't nearly as sure, but she was getting there. It was hard to believe she wasn't enough woman for him after a night like the one they had spent. It *had* been special.

But she was still uncertain. No matter how good the sex was, they wouldn't be spending their lives in bed. And how long would it last if love wasn't what made it so special to begin with? But she did love him…was that enough?

She took a shower, dressed in a fresh pair of jeans and neon-pink T-shirt, clothes appropriate for a nanny to wear. Children liked bright colors and so did she…but she didn't think Princess Therese would be caught dead in the bargain rack jeans and neon colored shirt. How could Tomasso believe she would fit into his life?

There was no doubting he did, but how could he? Was she wrong to be so unsure of herself and her place by his side?

Those two questions played a nonstop litany in her mind as she went to join him and the now awake children in the main cabin. They were eating breakfast at the table Tomasso had been working on before. Gianni was beside Tomasso. Anna sat across from them, an open spot beside her.

Maggie slid into it. "Good morning, everyone…or is it afternoon already in Beijing?"

"More like the wee hours of the morning, but it is the next day," Tomasso said.

Anna reached up and gave Maggie a childish kiss on her cheek in greeting. "You slept a long time. We got ready and everything and you didn't even notice."

"I must have been very tired."

"You need to eat your breakfast, Maggie," Gianni said. "Papa says we're going to land soon."

The flight attendant must have had the same thought because she put a plate of fruit with a bagel in front of Maggie.

Maggie thanked her and then returned the children's smiles without looking at Tomasso. "How exciting. I wonder if it will take long to get out of the airport. I've never been to China."

Anna squirmed as if she wanted to jump up and rush around the cabin. "Papa's been lots of times, huh, Papa?"

"Yes. I have. I will enjoy showing all of you around."

Maggie looked at him then, blushing under his quizzical stare.

"Did you sleep well?" he asked.

"Uh…yes. Very well. Thank you."

"Very soundly, too, I think."

Because she hadn't noticed him leaving the bed? He had her there. It felt strange to know that he had watched her sleeping, almost as intimate as what they had shared the night before. Had she mumbled his name in her sleep?

She'd been known to do so before, according to her former roommates and charges.

"Yes, Maggie…you didn't hear us come in and wake

you and Papa up." Gianni gave her a considering look. "Papa said he had to share your bed because he's too long to sleep in a chair. But you're not too long, are you?"

"But we didn't wake Maggie up," Anna pointed out. "Only Papa. How come you didn't wake up, Maggie?"

Maggie didn't know which child to respond to first, much less what to say. She looked to Tomasso for help, but the expression of intimate humor in his eyes only added to her embarrassed confusion.

"She told you, she was tired," Gianni said, saving Maggie from having to answer that question at least. "I bet she had jet lag."

Maggie wasn't about to explain to the child that jet lag came after travel, not during it, because Anna said, "Oh. I don't have jet lag."

"Me, neither, but how come you were in Papa's bed?" Gianni asked again.

She hadn't been in Tomasso's bed. She'd been in her own and he'd decided to share it, but she doubted Gianni would appreciate the nuances of the situation. "I…uh…it was more comfortable, and it's a big enough bed for two people to share."

"I thought only mommies and daddies shared beds," Anna said ingenuously.

"That's not right," Gianni said with a puckered frown on his forehead. "Zia Therese and Zio Claudio have the same bedroom, but they don't have any kids."

"But they're married," Anna pronounced. "It's the same as them being a mommy and a daddy."

"And so shall Maggie and I be just as soon as it can be arranged."

"You're getting married?" Anna breathed in awe.

"Yes," he said firmly, his blue gaze confident.

"Tomasso!" Maggie squeaked, unprepared for the frontal attack, though why it should surprise her, she didn't know.

This Scorsolini prince had already shown he could be ruthless when pursuing an objective, and that was exactly what she had become to him.

CHAPTER TEN

HER protest was drowned out by the delighted shouts from Anna and Gianni.

"So, you do not mind having Maggie for a mother now?" Tomasso asked his son.

Gianni's eyes so like his papa's were glowing. "No, Papa. You told me that if *Maggie* were our mama, she would be even better than a nanny because she would still watch over us and play with us, but she would stay with us forever."

He'd been talking to the children about her…about what kind of mom she would be?

"It's true, isn't it, Maggie?" Gianni asked, the worry evident in his voice.

For once, he had not accepted his papa's words as gospel, but she could tell he wanted to.

"If I were your mother, I would want to be with you just as I am now and no, I would not go away."

"What about what you told Zia Therese…about leaving in two years?"

"What I told Her Highness would not apply if I married your father instead of being your nanny," she said carefully, making no promises and yet feeling the inevitability of her future wash over her despite her caution.

Anna's eyes filled with tears and she threw herself at Maggie, hugging her around her neck so tight Maggie could barely breathe. "I wanted you to be my mama so bad. I love you, Maggie."

Maggie felt moisture burn her own eyes and she hugged Anna back with fierce affection. "I love you, too, sprite, both you and Gianfranco."

She didn't know how it happened, but Gianni ended up squeezed up next to her in her seat hugging her and Tomasso looked on with a smug benevolence that made Maggie want to scream. She'd never said she would marry him. They'd made love, but that wasn't a serious, full-on commitment in today's world. Was it?

Only, how could she disappoint these two precious children?

She couldn't deny that his preemptive action was getting her what she wanted most in the world, Tomasso and his children…a family of her own. And as scary as that was, as much as she knew this unequal relationship was setting herself up for pain, the joy unfurling in her heart said it was also a dream come true.

Even so, he had no business making that sort of decision on her behalf.

Which was exactly what she planned to tell him now that they were settled into their hotel suite, conspicuous in its design because it only had two bedrooms and a sitting room. The small contingent of personal security that had traveled to China with them had an adjoining suite and Tomasso's pilot and flight attendant were in rooms on another floor.

She left the children playing a game of Snakes and Ladders in the main room and followed Tomasso into his bedroom where he was unloading his briefcase onto the bed.

"Where exactly am I supposed to sleep? Anna's bed is hardly big enough to share."

He looked up, his expression neutral. "It does not seem to matter how luxurious the accommodation in China, it is difficult to find anything with a lot of space or large beds."

"I notice your bed is oversized."

"And it is a good thing, or we would not both fit in it comfortably."

"I am not sharing the bed with you."

He stopped what he was doing and faced her, his blue gaze probing hers. "Of course you will. Where else would you sleep?" His lips tilted in a mocking half smile. "As you pointed out, Anna's bed is too narrow to share."

"In my own room."

"There is not another bedroom in the suite."

"Then rent me my own quarters like you did the flight attendant. Surely I deserve at least her consideration."

"This is not about consideration, Maggie. You belong in my bed. We settled this last night."

"We didn't settle anything of the kind. And we certainly didn't *talk* about where you expected me to sleep once we got here. I would have remembered that conversation."

"After what transpired between us, there was no need to discuss it, surely?"

"You planned this all along, didn't you?" she accused. "You can't even use last night as an excuse because you had the rooms booked before we ever got onto the plane."

"What crime exactly are you charging me with?" he asked in an all too reasonable voice.

Which only made her angrier. She didn't feel reasonable. She felt maneuvered. "Trying to force my hand. I did not agree to come along on this trip as your bit on the side."

"We are going to be married. Do not ever speak of yourself in such disparaging terms again."

"Who says we're getting married?"

"I do."

"Here's a newsflash for you—it takes two cooperative parties to enter into a marriage in this day and age."

"You agreed to our marriage last night with your body and you did not deny it with your mouth this morning."

"I knew it!"

"Knew what?"

"You were using the children as a lever to force me into agreeing to marry you. You knew I couldn't say no to them. That's sneaky, not to mention cruel to them if you are wrong. What happened to you not making promises you weren't sure you could keep?"

"I am not wrong." He looked thoroughly offended she could accuse him of such a thing. "You gave yourself to me last night...you sealed your fate and my own."

"We had sex! I did not make a lifelong vow!"

"In giving yourself to me, you did that very thing. It is the way you are made."

She stared at him, poleaxed by what he had said and how well he knew her. He was right, darn it. She did feel committed to him now, in a way she hadn't after the dream-to-reality incident. But it wasn't just because they'd made love. Although that was a big part of it. She'd also admitted to herself that she loved him.

His calculating blue gaze said he'd known her agreement to make love with him had meant more than only that before she had. That he had in fact known before touching her last night that once she gave her body to him, she would feel fully committed.

He'd seduced her into wanting to accept his offer of a

marriage of convenience and it was only her stubborn pride that held her back from verbal agreement.

Furious at being maneuvered so neatly, she spun on her heel. "I'm not sleeping in here with you."

She never got her hand on the doorknob.

He grabbed her shoulders and pulled her back around to face him with implacable hands. "What is the matter with you? Why are you so angry? I am not such a bad catch, am I?"

She ignored that last bit of conceit. "You mean besides the fact that you obviously intended to seduce me once we got here?"

That really rankled on top of everything else because it said that, despite what she'd believed the night before, he'd never intended to honor her choices.

He sighed, the sound harsh and his expression austere. "Let us take care of that misconception. I changed the room arrangements when we arrived at the hotel. I am a very wealthy man—I do not have problems doing things like that. The hotel was happy to adjust our reservations to my new requirements. However, prior to our arrival, they had us booked for a suite with a room connected for you to stay in and a suite across the hall for the security team. After last night, I assumed—perhaps arrogantly—that you would willingly share my bed. It is precisely where I want you to be, so I arranged our sleeping accommodations accordingly."

"Oh."

"Better?"

"A little." A lot, actually, but she wasn't about to tell him so. "That doesn't alter the fact that you told the children we are getting married without my consent. I don't like being railroaded."

"I did not. You gave your consent."

She gasped. "I *never* said I'd marry you."

"As we both know and I have already stated…you said it loud and clear with your body, *tesoro mio*."

"But—"

"There are no buts, Maggie. Your body speaks more honestly than your lips."

"I don't lie."

"Then tell me you do not want to be my wife…my lover…my woman. Say these words with your lips and I *will* believe you."

She stared at him. She opened her mouth, but no sound came out. She couldn't say the words, not and tell the truth. She settled for a truth that was every bit as important, at least to her. "I don't want you to hurt me again."

"I did not intend to hurt you six years ago, and will not do so again."

She didn't believe him. How could he avoid hurting her when he'd been so oblivious the first time around? Wasn't it inevitable, given she loved him and he didn't love her?

"What happens when another Liana comes along, someone more suited to being a princess?" She looked down at her T-shirt and jean-clad self. "Look at me. I don't fit the mold."

He squeezed her shoulders, his face hard. "What you look like does not dictate who you are."

"This from a man who dated more beautiful women during his college years than most men do in a lifetime?"

"I have grown up since then."

"It's not just a matter of maturity." She wished it was, because no one would accuse this man of being childish.

"I assure you, it is."

"But look at the woman your brother married. I'm nothing like Princess Therese. She grew up around royalty, she's sophisticated and classy to her toenails. For goodness sake, she looks like a poster child for haute couture, not to mention she should be on the list of the Hundred Most Beautiful Women in the world. She's exactly what a princess should be."

"So, let her take you shopping for a new wardrobe if it will make you feel more confident, but it is the woman under your delectable skin I wish to marry."

"How can you?"

He bent down until their lips almost met. "We are great together, Maggie. You are fantastic for my children, good for me. How can I not?"

Then he kissed her and she melted into him with disturbing ease. If she didn't marry the man, she was going to end up being his clandestine lover and probably a pregnant one at that. She had no self-restraint where he was concerned. And no sense of self-preservation, either.

Like the first time, they had forgotten to use a condom last night…during any of the multiple times they had made love.

"You didn't use anything," she whispered as his mouth slid from her lips to explore along her jaw line.

"What?" he asked, his voice satisfyingly husky.

She forced herself to focus on her thoughts, not the sensations shivering through her body. "Was it on purpose?"

"Was what on purpose?"

"Not using any protection again last night when we made love."

He stopped kissing her and reared back, glaring down at her. "What did you say?"

"I want to know if you purposefully made love to me without protection because you thought if I got pregnant, it would be easier to get your way."

His blue gaze narrowed consideringly and then an

expression that looked like guilt flitted across his gorgeous features.

"You did," she said, outraged. "You made love to me on purpose with the intent to increase the risk of pregnancy."

"I did not."

"You looked guilty."

He glared down at her, his gaze hard as granite now. "I do not lie."

"But just now—that look—"

"Was me feeling damn guilty for being so irresponsible with your body, but that alone is a strong indicator we need to marry."

"How do you figure that?"

"I have no control when I am touching you. You have none, either, or you would have thought of it. Sooner or later, I *would* make you pregnant. I would prefer that be within the bonds of marriage."

"If I married you, it wouldn't be like it was with Liana."

"I am aware of that."

"I mean, I wouldn't tolerate the workaholic habits. I would expect you to put me and the children first at least ninety percent of the time and you'd spend a lot of time making up for the other ten percent."

"And would you make that easier for me by traveling on occasion with me as you have done this time?"

"If it means spending more time together as a family, yes. But I'm not the only one who will be doing the compromising. You will be around for important events like birthdays and school plays, which means if a business emergency arises, you consider your children and my feelings of more importance than making another million."

He smiled and she glared. "I mean it. You would have to promise me before I agreed to marriage."

"I believe I can do that."

"You'd have to do more than believe…you would have to follow through. I would also expect you to take normal weekends off as well as at least two family vacations a year, and we spend all major holidays like Christmas and Easter together as a family."

"That is a Scorsolini family tradition, but I'm confident most families only take one vacation per year."

"You're a prince, you can do as you like. You have a high-pressure job and the requirements of your station. At least twice a year, I would expect you to retreat from the world and let the children and I know that we are the most important people in your life." She couldn't believe she was demanding all these things, but she knew what made a strong family and she also knew that if he gave it, their marriage actually had a chance at survival.

"Very well. Two family vacations a year and you in my bed every night."

"Bed is fairly important to you, isn't it?"

"This is true, but I think you enjoy yourself when you are there, too."

"I do now."

He grinned. "So, we are agreed?"

She thought of the alternative. Life without him…again. Life without Anna and Gianni.

"Yes. I will marry you."

Their kiss was interrupted by two childish voices wanting to know why the people on the television didn't speak either English or Italian.

The next two days were hectic for Tomasso, who had back to back meetings late into the evening both days, but on the third one, he took the morning off to take her and the children shopping in marketplace.

She was awed by the way he interacted with the Chinese shop keepers, using his fluent Mandarin to bargain with them for toys that caught the children's eyes and a yellow silk kimono that caught his. It was beautiful, with pink and white flowers embroidered all over it. He asked her if she liked it and she nodded. That was when the bargaining began in earnest.

It went back and forth and at one point the shopkeeper slapped his arm, saying something sharply in Mandarin. Tomasso merely smiled and held his hand out with some money in it.

She cracked a smile herself, shook her head, but took the money and gave him the kimono.

He presented it to Maggie with a flourish that made the shopkeeper laugh and say something to the others around her that had them offering up several items obviously meant for women.

"What did she say?" Maggie asked.

"A fair flower like you deserved many gifts and that I should not stop at a mere kimono, especially one I got for such a good price."

"I really don't need presents at all. You have given me so much more that really matters."

"Yes?" he asked in an obvious bid for a compliment. She grinned, liking that his temperament expressed such a need. It showed a tiny bit of vulnerability. "You've given me two incredible children that will bless me all my life."

"And a lifetime with me, do not forget."

"I'm not likely to," she said dryly, but she reached up and kissed his cheek to show she really did appreciate him.

He went still, his blue gaze going dark.

"What's the matter?"

"That is the first time you have kissed me of your own accord."

She shrugged. "I'm shy."

"Not with the children. You hug and kiss them all the time."

But she was shy with him. Even in bed, only responding when he orchestrated lovemaking, never initiating herself. She was still having a hard time believing he wanted her for his wife, for his lifelong mate. She hadn't thought he'd notice her behavior, but he had.

"I'll hug and kiss you more freely after we are married."

"You promise, as I promised to put the family first?"

"Yes."

"It is a deal then."

"That is really important to you, isn't it?"

"Yes." He didn't say anything else, but she didn't expect him to. Not in front of the children.

But she couldn't help wondering if Liana had not been an affectionate woman. Maybe there were things she could give Tomasso that a more beautiful woman would not.

They were looking at traditional Chinese wedding finery in a shop that ended up being next to a tea house he'd taken them to for some traditional Chinese tea when he asked, "How big a wedding do you want?"

"I get to choose? I thought all royal weddings had to be huge and very, very traditional."

He fingered a headpiece made of gold, while the shop owner's gray-haired wife helped a giggling Anna try one on. "Do you want the pageantry of a royal wedding?"

"You mean I really have a choice?"

Gianni made a war cry and sliced through the air with a sword he'd found on the far wall. Maggie gasped and would have lunged for him, but the elderly owner of the shop was already there, showing Gianni how to hold the traditional sword and speaking to the little boy in broken English that seemed to mesmerize him.

Tomasso cupped her neck, his thumb brushing along her jaw. "Yes. You always have a choice, Maggie. I will not force you to do things that make you uncomfortable."

"Says the man who insisted I attend his father's birthday celebration as part of my job."

"I did not wish to be away from you for two days."

"That's sweet." And comforting.

"I am far from sweet."

Why did men always take issue with that word when applied to themselves? "What are you? Sour as a lemon?"

He leaned down and whispered into her ear, "I'm hot like lava and all I want to do right now is burn you."

She shuddered. He could do things with his voice that she was sure other men would never achieve with even a nighttime of touching. "Let's…um…get back to the small wedding idea."

He smiled, his expression knowing. He was obviously taking no chances on her backing out of his marriage of convenience and planned to keep her sexually enthralled until then. Besides, she had a sneaking suspicion that the man knew exactly how he affected her and he just plain liked knowing it, too.

"So, you would prefer something small?" he asked.

"Yes."

"I am glad."

"Don't you like big crowds?" She couldn't imagine that being the case, but why else would it matter?

"A small wedding means we can marry sooner."

"You aren't seriously afraid I'll change my mind, are you?"

"I will not let you."

"Papa said you're staying with us forever," Gianni piped up, making her aware that he had crossed the small shop to stand near them, the sword strapped to his waist and dragging on the floor.

"I am," she quickly affirmed having heard a tremulous doubt in the little boy's voice that broke her heart.

"Papa, Maggie, look at that," Anna cried and pointed to a man walking by the open doorway to the shop wearing a digital billboard on his head advertising a local restaurant.

They all cracked up while the old shopkeeper shook his head. China had changed since his days as a boy. Technology was everywhere, but he still had family in the country who had never ridden in a car.

Beijing was such a different place to any she'd ever visited before. The dull roar of copious voices was everywhere…the only sense of solitude to be found in their hotel suite. Even there, the sense of being surrounded by humanity remained in the knowledge the hotel was hemmed in on all sides by buildings of steel and glass, filled with people going about their business.

They ate a late lunch at The Emperor's Daughter's House, a restaurant that catered to executives and wealthy tourists. It was housed in the home of the last emperor's daughter, its historic flavor and ambience impressive even to the children. Young women dressed in the formal apparel of an earlier century danced for the patrons of the restaurant while more food than any family could eat in a week was repeatedly replenished on the round table at which they sat.

Tomasso had to leave them at the hotel while he went to yet another meeting, but both she and the children were content to be left behind, more than ready for a break from the constant noise and crowds.

She was sleeping when he finally made it back to the

hotel that night, but she woke when he climbed into the bed and gave a husky growl of appreciation upon finding her naked. For the past two nights, she'd worn her nightie only to have him strip it off of her in the heat of passion.

Remembering his desire for her to show him more affection, she'd decided to leave it off as an open invitation.

Apparently it was one he appreciated. She turned to him and initiated a hot, openmouthed kiss that led to other things that lasted into the wee hours of the morning.

The next day he surprised her and the children by taking them to the Forbidden City, where they toured the many temples, including the Temple of Heaven. He told her it was reputed the last Emperor had worshipped the Christian God, Yahweh, there.

As they walked from temple to temple women of every nationality watched Tomasso with hungry eyes, but he noticed none of them. His gaze never even paused to rest for a few seconds on the most beautiful and exotic.

Would it be the same back in Isole dei Re?

She could only hope.

They stayed in Beijing for two more days before returning to Diamante. Once there, Tomasso called his family to tell them the news of his impending second marriage. She and Tomasso agreed to go to Scorsolini Island before the birthday festivities began so the family could get to know Maggie better.

From what she could tell, none of them had expressed dismay at the prospect of Principe Tomasso Scorsolini marrying his nanny. But that didn't mean they accepted it without question. They could be waiting to express their disapproval until she and Tomasso arrived in Lo Paradiso, the capital city of Isole dei Re.

She wouldn't be surprised. What king wanted his son to marry his children's nanny—a woman who had been his own part-time housekeeper in the past?

CHAPTER ELEVEN

MAGGIE entered the palace in Lo Paradiso for the second time. Located smack in the center of Isole dei Re's capital city, its grandeur was every bit as awe inspiring as it had been on her first visit.

The cavernous marble entryway echoed with the sounds of the children's joyous laughter as they hurtled toward the private reception rooms. The Scorsolini family was very close. The kind of family Maggie had longed for since her parents' deaths. Here, uncles, aunt and grandfather all doted on Gianfranco and Annamaria.

She had yet to meet the youngest brother, Marcello, but the children spoke glowingly of him and with obvious affection.

Tomasso led her into the family reception room where he introduced her to his father. King Vincente had the same cobalt-blue eyes as Tomasso, but he looked at Maggie with an expression that seared her soul and tested her for worthiness. Her smile of greeting slipped from her lips.

His eldest son, Prince Claudio, was equally intimidating, his dark eyes fixed on her with an unfathomable expression as Maggie and Tomasso sat down on a small sofa covered in rich brocade. The children flanked their grandfather on the other sofa and Prince Claudio and Princess Therese were seated in Queen Anne style arm chairs upholstered in a complementary brocade to the one on the sofas.

The room was obviously meant to feel warm and cozy, but its size and the uncertain emotions of the occupants made Maggie feel like she was in a judge's chamber rather than the family reception room.

Only Princess Therese smiled at her, reaching out to squeeze Maggie's hand as if they were old friends. "I am so glad you and Tomasso are to be married. Your connection with the children was uncanny from the moment you all met. I remember telling Tomasso so on the phone when he asked if you'd taken the position. But now I understand."

"And what do you understand, Therese?" King Vincente asked.

"They knew each other before. Maggie saw bits of Tomasso in the children and was naturally drawn to them because of it."

"You think so?" Prince Claudio asked, sounding unconvinced himself.

Feeling like she should stand up for her obvious ally, Maggie said, "You're right, you know. Tomasso is the only other person in my life I connected to as quickly and as completely as I have with Anna and Gianni."

"If this is true, then why have we never met you before? This friendship my son told me about did not extend to introducing you to his family and for six years, you have been completely out of his life."

"I did not want Maggie to know I was a prince," Tomasso interrupted before she could reply. "It was important to me to go through college and graduate school on my own merits, not the cachet associated with my family's name."

"But if she was your friend…" Claudio's voice trailed off, the implication plain.

She had not been the close friend Tomasso claimed if he had kept his true identity from her.

"Sometimes we keep things from even the dearest people in our lives for reasons others might not understand." Princess Therese spoke up again. "Tomasso made his choice about that six years ago, but it is hardly Maggie's fault, nor should you and Vincente expect her to explain it."

"How many times have I told you to call me Papa?" the king scolded his daughter-in-law.

She merely smiled, a sadness flickering in her eyes. Maggie wondered if the others saw it.

"I told Maggie you would welcome her. Was I mistaken?" Tomasso asked in a voice that chilled the room.

"Nonno, don't you like Maggie?" Anna asked, her lower lip quivering. "I love her. She's going to be my mama."

"She promised, Nonno. You can't make her go away," Gianni said in childish desperation, his small face going red with anger. "I won't let you and neither will my papa!"

He jumped up and dashed around the large square coffee table in the center of the sitting arrangement to throw himself at his father. "You won't let Nonno send Maggie away, will you?"

Tomasso hugged his son, his eyes flinty hard and fixed on his father. "No. Now calm yourself, Gianfranco. You have nothing to fear from this family who loves you."

Anna must have moved when Gianni did because she climbed into Maggie's lap and hugged her neck. "I do love you, Maggie. I want you for my mama."

Maggie hugged the small body close and had to bite back a sigh. The situation had gone far enough and was helping no one. "It's all right, Anna. No one is trying to make me go away."

"But Papa got mad. I could tell."

Maggie did sigh then. "Yes, I think everyone could, but there was no reason for him to be mad. Your grandfather and uncle are only asking questions because they don't know me."

"When they do know you, they will love you like I do," Anna said with confidence.

"I am sure you are right, little one," Princess Therese added. "I like Maggie very much, and I am an excellent judge of character."

Her words were obviously directed at her husband and his father and both men frowned in receipt of the subtle criticism.

"Perhaps you can tell us something about yourself," King Vincente said to Maggie in an obvious bid to smooth the troubled waters around him.

Prince Claudio gave her a considering look. "Actually, Tomasso mentioned you many times to me when you worked for him six years ago. You kept his life peaceful."

"Yes, he mentioned that," Maggie said wryly. "Good domestic help is hard to come by." She'd learned that much while working as a nanny for two wealthy families. "It was worth mentioning he had some, I suppose."

"I was under the impression he enjoyed more than the fact you kept the house clean and fed him."

"We were good friends," Tomasso inserted. "I told you this."

"But it was not a friendship that lasted after the working relationship." Though it was a statement, Prince Claudio made it sound like a question.

"College friendships are often like that. How many friends from your days at University do you keep in contact with?" she asked him.

"Very few," Prince Claudio admitted.

"There, you see," Princess Therese said. "You are looking for anomalies that do not exist."

Prince Claudio shrugged and then focused his dark-eyed gaze on his younger brother. "If you knew who Maggie was when you asked Therese to hire her, it stands to reason that you planned to marry her all along."

"Yes."

"Not quite," Maggie said.

"What then?" the king asked.

"You know your son…he had a plan."

"What kind of plan," Princess Therese asked, her eyes lit with curiosity.

"He planned to test me out for suitability first," Maggie said with a straight face.

"You cannot be serious!" Princess Therese exclaimed.

"But I am."

King Vincente nodded his approval. "That was wise."

Typical Scorsolini male reaction. Maggie choked on a sound of amused resignation and winked at Princess Therese who looked ready to burst out laughing.

"Your test was short-lived," Prince Claudio pointed out.

Tomasso shrugged with the same casual arrogance his brother had shown seconds earlier. "It did not take me long to determine that Maggie was all that I remembered."

"I see."

Tomasso went into an embarrassing litany of her praises, aided and abetted by Anna and Gianni. If his family didn't see that her Girl Scout-like qualities were her biggest appeal to a man looking for a *peaceful marriage*, she did. He even mentioned a desire she'd voiced to establish a preschool system in Isole dei Re.

"That is an interesting idea, but will you not be too busy caring for my son and grandchildren to see to such a task?"

"It isn't something that has to happen all at once, Your Highness. I would probably start with a preschool near Tomasso's home on Diamante."

"Even so, that sort of endeavor would most certainly conflict with you looking after Tomasso and the children."

"Your son is an adult," retorted Maggie. "He doesn't need me looking after him as if he wasn't, and I would never neglect Anna and Gianni in order to see to the needs of other children. They are now and will continue to be my top priority, but that does not preclude me taking an interest in anything else." It seemed to her that for all the times Tomasso had told her this was the twenty-first century, someone needed to remind his father of that fact.

The king surprised her by smiling with obvious approval. "Thank you. It is my belief that you could not have engendered such strong devotion in my grandchildren without just cause, but I wanted to make sure. Forgive me if you felt under the gauntlet. Some women do not share your priorities. Both a husband and children can be very hurt by such neglect."

It suddenly occurred to Maggie that Tomasso's marriage to Liana had probably been painful for the other Scorsolinis to deal with. She had been a selfish woman who put her own pleasure at the forefront of her priorities and hurt many people because of it.

"I would never let that happen. Please believe me."

"I do believe you. Therese tells me that you took no days off while Tomasso was away on business, even though the staff at the villa stood ready to care for the children if you wished to do so."

Tomasso gave her a pointed look as if to say, "See, you didn't really want days off anyway."

She shrugged, but had to stifle a smile. The man really liked being right. "I enjoy their company."

"And that of my son?" the king asked.

"Father," Tomasso said sternly, but his father wasn't intimidated.

"Do you love my son?"

Tomasso's frown was now hard enough to crush diamonds. "That is not a question that needs asking. I am content with this marriage. Therefore, you should be, too."

King Vincente shook his head. "You do not think the question relevant? I disagree." He turned to face her again. "I ask you once more…do you love my son?"

Maggie had a choice. She could lie and save her pride, or she could tell the truth. She'd never been any good at lying, so really, she had no choice at all.

"Yes, I do," she said quietly, refusing to be humiliated by the one-sided nature of their relationship, but there was no denying the slice of pain that went through her. "I also love the children."

He hadn't asked, but she thought it was important to say so, for Gianni and Anna's sake if nothing else.

Tomasso went still beside her and she avoided meeting his eyes by smoothing Anna's hair though it hardly needed it.

"You loved him six years ago." It was the king again, continuing to probe the incision he had just made in the protective membrane around her heart.

It hurt and she sucked in a pain-filled breath no one else in that room would understand. "I…that isn't any of your business."

"I agree." Therese stood. "Not only are you poking into things that do not concern you, you are doing it in a venue that is entirely inappropriate." She gave a pointed look to the two children who were listening with rapt attention to the conversation of the adults.

"You have already upset your grandchildren, you have offended your second son, and you have embarrassed a woman you should be calling daughter. I always knew the Scorsolini men were efficient, but that is taking overachievement to the extreme in my opinion. Maggie, would you like to go to your room now?"

Before Maggie could nod, the king said, "I beg your pardon. It was not my intention to upset the children, or embarrass you."

"But you don't mind offending your son?" Maggie asked with no doubt misplaced humor, but she couldn't seem to stop herself.

The king's lips twitched and then he gave her a full-blown smile every bit as devastating as his son's. "I am used to offending my sons. They are strong men."

"I'm a strong woman, but I don't like being grilled on my feelings and I agree with Princess Therese that the children have been unnecessarily upset."

"I am sorry, little ones. You will forgive your *nonno*, will you not?" he asked with his arms outstretched.

Anna rushed to her grandfather to give him a hug and assure that all had been forgiven, but Gianni held back.

"Gianfranco?"

"Maggie is to be my mama."

"Yes."

"I love her, too."

"I can see that you do and it is commendable, *piccolo mio*."

"You aren't going to try to send her away?"

"No. She belongs with your family...with the Scorsolini family. Besides, as you pointed out, your father would hardly allow such a thing. He is easily as stubborn as your *nonno*."

Gianni nodded and then crossed to sit beside his grandfather again, taking the older man's hand in an affectionate gesture that moved Maggie. The Italian influence on this family was obvious and she liked it.

Princess Therese sat down again without looking at her husband who was watching her with a strange expression in his eyes.

She then gave her father-in-law a look that made him shift in his seat and turn to Maggie to say, "Tell me more about these preschools you think we need in Isole dei Re."

That signaled the end of her interrogation, and conversation flowed along less antagonistic lines after that. Now that he wasn't looking at her like she'd climbed out from under a rock or asking embarrassing questions, Maggie found Tomasso's father very charming and even likable. Prince Claudio was quiet, but apparently his concerns regarding the marriage had also been laid to rest.

However, Maggie was still relieved when Therese suggested she might like some time to relax and freshen up before dinner.

CHAPTER TWELVE

"We'll fly to Nassau tomorrow morning so we can do our shopping," Princess Therese said as she led Maggie from the reception room.

"That sounds wonderful. Thank you. I don't want to embarrass Tomasso at his father's birthday party by looking like the hired help, but my clothes budget has never run to designer originals."

Princess Therese laughed softly. "Most women's don't and you have nothing to fear in that regard. With the right connections, clothing is an easy matter to see to. The outer appearance of a woman can be manipulated to fit any occasion, but your inner character is irreplaceable."

"I have told her this, but perhaps she will listen to you."

Therese turned to face Tomasso who had followed them out of the reception room. "Perhaps those are not the words she needs to hear from you."

Tomasso frowned and Maggie felt a sudden and horrible urge to cry. The words Therese was talking about were no more likely to pass his lips today than they had six years ago.

"What time are you two flying out tomorrow?" he asked, ignoring the princess's comment.

"Seven in the morning, but I had considered flying out

tonight. Only I thought it might be too much for Maggie after the journey here."

"The helicopter trip was less than an hour. I'm hardly jetlagged," Maggie said with a smile, the thought of getting away from Tomasso for a short while appealing in the extreme.

"Perhaps we could fly out after dinner then," Princess Therese said. "It will give us a full day of shopping tomorrow and the next day before I have to return to attend to my duties for the party."

"That sounds perfect."

"You can't need two days of shopping to come up with one outfit," Tomasso said with an obvious displeasure she could not understand.

"Don't be silly, Tomasso," Therese said. "We will be outfitting Maggie for more than one occasion. As your fiancé, soon to be your wife, she will need an extensive wardrobe. We can add to it later, but we must fit her with the basics immediately so that she will not feel conspicuous or uncomfortable moving within your social and business circles."

Maggie appreciated Princess Therese's understanding and her smile told the other woman so.

"Perhaps I should come with you then."

"No, thank you. Men, particularly those with strong opinions and the certainty they are always right, are not a welcome addition on a shopping trip of this nature."

Before Tomasso could argue, Claudio came into the hall and said he wanted his brother's opinion on a business matter.

"He does not want you out of his sight for two days," Therese said with interest as she led Maggie up the marble staircase.

"I don't know why."

"He is possessive."

"It seems to be a family trait."

"Yes, but you will not hear Claudio offering to come to the States with us to go shopping in order to remain in my company."

"I suppose that in your positions you are used to being separated for the sake of your duties."

Therese stopped in front of a large, ornately carved door that matched the other dozen or so lining the long marble hallway. "Yes."

Maggie sensed a sadness in the other woman she was too sensitive to address. "I really appreciate you taking me under your wing like this, Princess Therese."

"It is my pleasure. We are family, Maggie. And please, you must stop calling me Princess. Therese will do nicely."

She nodded, but said, "I don't think I'll ever call King Vincente anything else."

Therese's soft laughter followed Maggie into the huge suite she was apparently supposed to share with Tomasso.

In some ways, the family had moved very much into the twenty-first century. Her mother, had she lived, would never have allowed Maggie and a soon-to-be son-in-law to sleep together under her roof before the wedding. Maggie wasn't sure she felt comfortable with doing so now. At least at Tomasso's home, she had her own suite…even if he came to her bed the nights he did not carry her to his.

She took a long bath in the en suite, soaking and thinking for so long she had to rush to get ready for dinner. She pulled her hair up in a mass of curls on top of her head that she didn't have time to tame. It didn't look too bad, but she would have preferred a smoother, more conservative do.

Tomasso arrived to change into a suit as she was pulling on one of the dresses she'd bought to wear while attending social functions with her previous employers. It was simple, elegant and black. A far cry from the bright colors she usually wore, it made her feel like she blended into her surroundings, which is exactly what she had wanted to do on those occasions.

She didn't feel appreciably different tonight.

"Did you have a nice rest?" he asked as he peeled off his dress shirt and slacks to don a fresh pair of trousers and new, crisply ironed shirt.

"I took a long soak."

His eyes heated to indigo. "I would like to have joined you. I spent the afternoon in business meetings with my brother while our father played *nonno* to the hilt with the children."

"I'm sure you enjoyed yourself. You thrive on the stress of your job."

"As does Claudio, but I would still have rather been making love to you in the bath."

She rolled her eyes, her cheeks going cherry pink. "Don't you think of anything else?"

Maybe the seduction thing wasn't all for her benefit. The man was definitely oversexed.

He knotted his tie. "You know I do, but I cannot help it if your passion is so addictive that I struggle to get thoughts of you out of my mind."

She turned away, the words too close to real emotion when she knew there was none behind them for her to handle. "Therese changed our flight to nine this evening."

Suddenly his hands were on her waist and his lips pressed against her exposed nape. "I will miss you, Maggie. Will you miss me?"

"You know I will."

"Because you love me?"

She'd wondered when that would come up. There was

no use denying it when she had already admitted her feelings in front of his family. "Yes."

"I am glad."

She wanted to ask why it mattered, but he'd turned her to kiss her and when he was done, she was in no condition to ask anything.

He finished dressing. Then he crossed the room and opened a safe in the wall from which he pulled out a narrow black velvet case. He handed it to her.

"What is this?"

"Open it and find out."

She did, revealing a long strand of perfectly shaped pearls each one an exact color match. "They're beautiful," she gasped.

"They will go nicely with your dress."

She pressed the box back into his hand. "I won't wear Liana's jewelry," she said as she backed away from him, her stomach tightening.

"They were not Liana's. Her tastes were far more flashy. These were my mother's."

"Why aren't they Therese's then?"

"My father gave pieces to both Claudio and myself when we came of age."

"You're sure Liana never wore it?"

"Quite sure."

"Okay." Realizing how ungracious that sounded she added, "I mean thank you very much. They really are beautiful. I'll take good care of them for you."

"They are yours now," he said in a voice that did not invite argument.

"Thank you."

"Would it matter so much if Liana had worn them?"

"Yes."

He nodded, his expression grave. "Then, be assured I will never give you anything that belonged to her before."

Including his heart. He'd already made that clear.

The trip to Nassau was a revelation for Maggie. Therese knew exactly where to go to get haute couture and she had an incredible eye for what would look good on Maggie. They shopped all morning and broke for lunch before starting again.

Tomasso called three times during the day. Once in the morning, once around lunch time and again a couple of hours later. The phone calls were brief and not at all romantic, but she liked getting them and smiled for a long time after each one. She and Therese got the bulk of their shopping done and left accessorizing for Day Two. When they returned to the hotel, Maggie had clothes for every occasion and a killer dress for the king's birthday bash.

She and Therese found out that despite the differences in their backgrounds, they had tons in common and spent a lot of time laughing. Which helped Maggie feel like maybe she would fit in with Tomasso's life. She certainly planned to try her best.

They used the pool's Jacuzzi to soak their aching muscles after the marathon shopping excursion.

Therese leaned against the wall of the hot tub, the water bubbling around her. "This feels so good."

Maggie nodded, groaning as the water jet hit her lower back. "Too good. I'm afraid I'll fall asleep down here."

"Better not. They'd catch you on the security cameras and sell the pictures to some sleazy tabloid with a story about boozing it up, or something equally vulgar."

"It isn't easy living life in the constant public eye, is it?"

"Luckily we don't get the press attention that Buckingham Palace does, but yes, you always have to be aware of the probability that you are being watched. Claudio would not be pleased if he knew we were relaxing here, even." She said it like the knowledge gave her some satisfaction and not for the first time Maggie wondered at the undercurrents in the royal couple's marriage.

"I thought the security team looked a little disgruntled when you said we were coming down here."

Therese shrugged. "You cannot live every moment pleasing everyone else."

"But you try, don't you?"

A look of sadness passed over the other woman's exotic features. "I have tried less lately."

"I think that's a good thing. It's too easy to be taken for granted when you're always trying to make life easier for everyone around you."

"Is that what happened six years ago with Tomasso? He took you for granted?"

"In a way, but I was his housekeeper…it came with my job description."

"But falling in love with him did not."

"No."

"It is hard to love a man who sees you as a convenience. It hurts."

Maggie agreed but the cell phone Tomasso had given her rang before she could say so. She smiled apologetically at Therese and then answered it. "Good evening, Tomasso."

"Hello, *bella mia*. Did you get your shopping finished?"

"The clothes. We are shopping for accessories tomorrow."

"You think it will take the full day?"

"I have no doubt about it."

He sighed. "I had hoped you would return early."

"It's nice to know I'm missed."

"I told you that you would be."

"It's still nice." Even if it was just that he missed having her in his bed.

"The children miss you as well. They wish to say good night."

"Of course, put them on." Anna wanted to know how soon Maggie would be returning and Gianni wanted to tell her all about their afternoon riding horses with their *nonno*.

Tomasso came back on the line. "I hear bubbling water."

"Therese and I are in the hot tub soaking our aching muscles."

"The public hot tub?"

"It's hardly public. It's the hotel hot tub."

"You are parading around the hotel in your swimsuits?" he asked as if women in his world didn't sunbathe regularly wearing nothing but a thong and some sunscreen.

"Hardly parading. We changed when we got to the pool area."

"I am surprised Therese encouraged you to do this."

"Does it really bother you?"

"Do you have security with you?"

"Yes."

"In that case, no. I would of course prefer to be there, but that is more for my own sake than my concern for yours."

"Therese thought Claudio might be upset."

"He is sometimes too aware of propriety."

"Because one day he will be king?"

"Probably. I have never asked." There were a few moments of silence and then he said, "My bed will be very lonely without you in it tonight."

"I assume the children are no longer in hearing distance."

"You are right. I have promised to come tuck them in when I finish speaking with you."

She sighed, holding the phone closer to her ear as if that could bring him closer to her as well. "I do miss you."

"Good."

She laughed softly. "Therese thinks we can arrange a small wedding in a week, two at the most. Is that too soon?"

"It is not soon enough, but it will do."

Warmth spread through her at the evidence he was eager for the marriage…whatever his reasons. "I suppose I had better go."

"What? Oh, yes…but first Claudio has just come in and would like to speak to Therese. Will you put her on?"

"Of course."

She handed the phone to Therese. "Prince Claudio wants to talk to you."

Therese looked at the phone with an odd expression and then took it. "Hello?"

She frowned. "I left my cell phone in the room." She paused. "I am in the hotel's hot tub on the pool level."

Maggie tried not to listen in on the rest of the conversation and concentrated on the relaxing feel of the bubbling water. She was almost dozing when Therese handed her back her phone.

"He is such a Neanderthal sometimes."

"That must run in the family, too."

They both laughed, Therese's green eyes filling with genuine mirth. "Yes, I believe it does."

They flew back to Lo Paradiso the next afternoon, the cargo hold full of Maggie and Therese's purchases.

She saw her family the minute the plane's outer door was opened. Tomasso waited with Anna in one arm and his other hand holding Gianni's. She fairly flew down the stairs to land against him. Within seconds, she was in the middle of a family hug that made her wonder if she might find true joy in her marriage despite the fact her fiancé did not love her.

She was almost positive of it late that night in the depths of his bed after he made such exquisite love to her that she lost touch with herself completely.

He grumbled the next morning when he found out that she had appointments with Therese's personal hair stylist, manicurist and a makeup artist. "Only promise me you will not let them cut your hair."

"The whole point is to get it cut."

"But I like it long."

"I'll ask them to keep the length and then style it, all right?"

He frowned, but nodded. "And not too much makeup. I do not wish to escort a Barbie doll to the party this evening."

"No wonder Therese insisted you not accompany us shopping. You would have been impossible."

"Perhaps, but I would not now be biting my nails in worry over what you chose to buy to wear tonight."

"You don't bite your nails."

"But I do worry."

"You're afraid I will embarrass you?" she asked.

He shook his head decisively. "Do not be stupid. I am concerned you will have bought a gown that shows the delectable figure I like to ogle in private to its best advantage. I am a possessive man."

"You're worried I'm going to look too sexy?" she asked in disbelief.

"I worry it cannot be helped, but with Therese's eye for style, it may be much worse than even I envision."

Her mind boggled that he could really be concerned about such a thing. "I guess you'll just have to wait and see, won't you?"

But several hours later, when she had been combed and

curried into a woman she almost didn't recognize, she was the nervous one. The stylist hadn't taken off much length, but he had styled her hair so that the natural curls fell around her face in sexy ringlets. The makeup artist had not used a lot of color, but enough to accentuate Maggie's eyes, making them seem almost silver rather than their true dull gray.

And the dress did show her figure off to perfection. It was off the shoulder and the burnt-orange of a sunset. It cupped her breasts and clung to her curves down her hips to her knees where it flared out to sweep the floor. Her heels gave her over two inches of height, but she still had to tilt her head to look Tomasso in the eye.

"What do you think?" She pirouetted for him.

"I think I would rather stay in this room and make love to you than introduce you to two hundred people who will insist on making me share your attention."

"Do you like it?"

"You look incredible. You will be the most beautiful woman present." He sounded like he really meant the words and the expression in his cobalt blue eyes said he believed what he was saying.

Her heart stuttered in her chest. "It isn't too bright?"

"I like you in bright colors."

"That's good. Therese insisted I buy lots of the colors I like to wear in the latest styles." She had said that it was important for Maggie to simply be a more put together version of herself, not try to emulate anyone else.

Maggie had liked that idea a lot.

"I am glad. I do not want you to change to fit what you believe my world to be." He pulled her close, taking care not to muss her appearance. "You are the woman I want. You are *real*, Maggie, and that is the way I want you to stay."

"I don't know how to be anything else."

"I am glad to know that."

They shared a smile that warmed her to her toes. And then he kissed her and she didn't mind in the least that she had to reapply her lipstick afterward.

She was very proud to enter the ballroom at his side a few minutes later.

He looked eye-catchingly yummy in his white formal suit, so much so that most of the female guests gave him at least one long glance. It was the same for his brothers though. Claudio and Marcello both received a great deal of female interest. Where Claudio seemed to ignore it, Marcello smiled and flirted with European charm, but still managed to hold the women swarming around him at a distance.

He had arrived from Italy earlier in the day and was as stunningly good-looking as his two older brothers. He shared the blue eyes of his father and Tomasso, but his complexion was darker and his hair was a lighter brown. Maggie wondered if his mother was a blonde. Some Italian women were.

Regardless, he took after his father in one unmistakable way…he shared the Scorsolini male pride and confidence. Which, Maggie realized, was every bit as attractive to women as the men's looks. There was no doubting that he and Tomasso received the lion's share of feminine attention in the room.

They were considered fair game: Marcello because he was, and Tomasso because the official announcement had not yet been made of his upcoming marriage. Maggie didn't know when it would be. No one had said anything to her about it, but she didn't really care it hadn't been made yet.

Watching the way some of the women were with Claudio, she knew even a wedding ring would not deter a certain type of female.

But as the night progressed and one gorgeous woman after another flirted with Tomasso, trying to prise him from Maggie's side, the urge to stake an unmistakable claim grew stronger. Tomasso wasn't shy about doing so, making it clear in subtle and not so subtle ways that they were a couple. Especially when other men asked her to dance, or spoke to her.

It was the fifth time the former had happened when Maggie had a revelation. She was not a princess, but that didn't stop other men in the room from noticing her. She was not as beautiful as Liana, but no one treated her as if she did not belong by Tomasso's side.

It was not merely the clothes, or the makeup, or the jewelry Tomasso had insisted she wear (more pieces passed down from his mother), nor was it her new haircut, though she loved it. It was that she *did* belong beside this man and somehow, most people realized that on an instinctive level. Women flirted, some gave her looks of envy, some even looked puzzled by his choice, but no one had implied by word or expression that she didn't belong.

She loved him. That was her claim on him. He might not love her, but he had made a commitment to her and his loyalty could not be questioned. His passion was as real as her love and his friendship was as precious to her as the passion.

This man was hers and he would be hers for the rest of both of their lives. And that would be enough. She would make it enough.

She turned to look at him, giving him a brilliant smile that made him stop speaking in midword and forget what he was going to say altogether.

The man he'd been talking to, a king from the Middle East no older than Tomasso, laughed. "There is no use in trying to hold a man's attention for a discussion of business when there is such a lovely woman close by to steal it."

Burnished red scorched along Tomasso's cheekbones, but he laughed and agreed.

The Middle Eastern king walked away and Tomasso turned to her. "What is it, Maggie?"

"What is what?"

"You are smiling."

"I like to smile."

"It is a special smile."

"Yes, it is. I love you, Tomasso."

The arm he had slung with casual possession around her waist tightened. "I know, and I am more pleased by that than I can say, but that still does not explain the smile, does it? You look so happy it is bursting out of you and yet I have had the impression from the moment you said yes, you had grave reservations about marrying me."

"I love you and that makes me so happy, I *am* bursting with it. Maybe I was a little worried about marrying you, but I'm not any more. I know you don't love me, not like that, and I thought that meant I would have to keep earning my place with you—no, please let me finish. I see now that unlike my years in foster care, I am not a temporary stop in your life. I'm going to be your wife until I die and I don't have to work at keeping that title, just love you and the children and we'll all be content. I don't know why it took so long, but I've just realized you are going to be a wonderful husband and I'm going to be Gianni and Anna's mom and have more children with you—and I'm very, very, very happy about all that."

His lips creased upward until his smile was as blinding as hers. "I am glad."

It was close to midnight when King Vincente called for everyone's attention. The room grew as quiet as one filled with over two hundred guests could.

"Tonight you celebrate my birthday with me and I thank you, but I have more to celebrate than another year of good health." He paused with the gift of a showman before beckoning Maggie and Tomasso over to him. When they stopped beside him, he smiled. "This lovely and very sweet woman has agreed to marry my son and our family rejoices in welcoming another Scorsolini princess."

Claudio handed him a velvet box, much like the one that had held the pearls Tomasso had given her. King Vincente opened it and revealed a small tiara which he placed on her head with gentle care before kissing both her cheeks. "Welcome to the family, daughter."

Applause broke out and it seemed like every person present wanted to know when the wedding was to take place, but that was one piece of information no one shared. Many guests said they'd been expecting an announcement after they'd seen the way Maggie and Tomasso looked at one another.

Maggie just grinned and accepted the congratulations with a peace she had not felt ever before in her life.

Tomasso had shown in too many ways to count that she really mattered to him. From the elaborate plan to get her back into his life to the way he acquiesced to her demands about his work hours so she would marry him to the way he made love to her so perfectly, he proved that she was special to him.

He might not love her, but he cared for her and he would be faithful and, when all was said and done, that was a lot more than a lot of men who said they loved their wives gave them.

Tomasso finally got Maggie alone and in his bed in the wee hours of the morning. He looked down at the beauty that shone from her rainwater eyes and was grateful she'd washed off her makeup.

"You looked beautiful tonight, but I prefer you without any artifice." His voice came out husky, which made sense because his throat felt like it was crowded with emotions he could not name.

"Thank you." There was that smile again. A sleepier version, but no less devastating to his heart.

"You are so perfect to me."

"You're perfect for me, too," she sighed.

She deserved all the words and somehow he was going to give them to her. He hadn't realized they were beating inside his heart, begging for expression until he'd looked down at her and seen the look of pure love glowing back at him earlier tonight. The love she gave him without asking for anything in return, and which made him see how much she deserved from him.

He'd thought love some kind of illusion, a weakness he did not want to give into.

But he understood now: it was not weak to love. It took strength, the kind that Maggie possessed. It took courage and he was not a man who would willingly fear anything.

"Six years ago, I loved you, but I was too stupid to realize it."

Her eyes opened wide and she sat up, clutching the sheet to her chest. "What?"

"You made my life perfect and I took that for granted. When I met Liana, I was smarting from your rejection, but I was also determined to keep our friendship, to have the best of both worlds. My head was turned by her outward beauty, I will not deny it, but I was devastated when you threatened to quit, and something inside me knew that if I did not allow you to walk away from our friendship later, my promises to Liana were in jeopardy. I was not mature enough to realize that should have clued me into the fact that what I felt for Liana was not love."

"It wasn't?"

"No. I loved you. How could I love another woman? Maybe Liana sensed that my feelings for her did not run as deep as they should have. Maybe that is why she spent so much time away from our family, but all I know is that I did not miss her when I worked. I miss you. Even a simple day in the office is enough to make me wish I were home, with you and the children."

"I…" Her voice trailed off as if she didn't know what to say.

"That first night, when I climbed into the bed with you…it was like a dream from my subconscious coming true. I cannot understand my own actions that night except that I finally had you where you were always meant to be and I think I was willing to do anything to keep you there."

"You said you didn't love me… I don't understand."

"I was being stupid again. Six years did not teach me that much, I guess."

"When did you realize?"

"I think I became aware that my feelings for you were far stronger than simple physical passion mixed with friendship when you were in Nassau shopping with Therese. I missed you so much and I craved talking to you on the phone. Claudio asked me if I was marrying you for the children's sake and I told him I was doing it for my own sake and understood at once how true that was, but I did not put the right words to the emotion until tonight…you smiled at me and all I wanted to do was carry you up here and make love to you until you screamed your pleasure."

Her eyes probed his. "That's lust, not love."

"Lust…or passion…it is a part of love, an easy part for a man to understand. The emotions, they are not so easy."

"And you feel the emotions?"

"So much that I would die if I were ever to lose you."

Her beautiful eyes filled with tears, but she smiled. "You will never lose me."

"And you will always have me," he vowed.

"Til death us do part."

"Until death…" He could not hold back and kissed her.

She melted against him like she always did, yielding to his body, giving herself so completely that an unfamiliar moisture burned his own eyes.

"I love you," he whispered against her lips as he entered her body minutes later.

"I love you," she said back to him with such conviction his soul stirred.

This woman was the true other half to himself and he would spend a lifetime thanking God for bringing her to him and showing her how very much he loved her.

HARLEQUIN *Presents*®

Welcome to a world filled with passion, romance and royals!

Royal Brides

The Scorsolini Princes: Proud rulers and passionate lovers who need convenient wives!

HIS ROYAL LOVE-CHILD
by Lucy Monroe

June 2006

Danette Michaels knew that there
would be no marriage or future as Principe Marcello
Scorsolini's secret mistress. When she wanted more, the affair
ended. Until a pregnancy test changed everything...

Other titles from this new trilogy by Lucy Monroe
THE PRINCE'S VIRGIN WIFE—May
THE SCORSOLINI MARRIAGE BARGAIN—July

If you enjoyed what you just read,
then we've got an offer you can't resist!

Take 2 bestselling
love stories FREE!

Plus get a FREE surprise gift!

Bedded by *Blackmail*

Forced to bed...then to wed?

He's got her firmly in his sights
and she has only one chance of
survival—surrender to
his blackmail...and
him...in his bed!

THE ITALIAN'S BLACKMAILED MISTRESS

by

Jacqueline Baird

On sale this June!

Coming Next Month

THE BEST HAS JUST GOTTEN BETTER!

#2541 HIS ROYAL LOVE-CHILD Lucy Monroe
Royal Brides

Danette Michaels knew that there would be no marriage, future or public acknowledgment as Principe Marcello Scorsolini's secret mistress. When she wanted more, the affair ended. Until a pregnancy test changed everything.

#2542 THE SHEIKH'S DISOBEDIENT BRIDE Jane Porter
Surrender to the Sheikh

He's a warrior who lives by the rules of the desert. When Sheikh Tair finds Tally has broken one of those sacred laws, he must act. Tally is kept like a slave girl, and her instinct is to flee, but as ruler, Tair must tame her. He knows he wants her—willing or not!

#2543 THE ITALIAN'S BLACKMAILED MISTRESS Jacqueline Baird
Bedded by Blackmail

For Max Quintano, blackmailing Sophie into becoming his mistress was simple: she'd do anything to protect her family from ruin—even give up her freedom to live in Max's Venetian palazzo. Now she's beholden to him, until she discovers exactly *why* he hates her so much.

#2544 WIFE AGAINST HER WILL Sara Craven
Wedlocked!

Darcy Langton is horrified when she finds herself engaged to arrogant, but sexy, businessman Joel Castille! But when Darcy makes a shocking discovery about her new husband, it's up to Joel to woo her back or risk losing his most valuable asset.

#2545 FOR REVENGE...OR PLEASURE? Trish Morey
For Love or Money

Jade Ferraro is a cosmetic surgeon, and Loukas Demakis is certain she's preying on the rich and famous of Beverly Hills to attract celebrity clients. He has no qualms about seducing information from Jade to uncover the truth.

#2546 HIS SECRETARY MISTRESS Chantelle Shaw
Mistress to a Millionaire

Jenna Deane is thrilled with her new job. Life hasn't been easy since her husband deserted her and their little daughter. But her new handsome boss expects Jenna to be available whenever he needs her. How can she tell him that she's a single mother?

HPCNM0506